FIRESTORM AT KOOKABURRA STATION

Books by Robert Elmer

PROMISE OF ZION

#1 / *Promise Breaker*
#2 / *Peace Rebel*
#3 / *Refugee Treasure*

ADVENTURES DOWN UNDER

#1 / *Escape to Murray River*
#2 / *Captive at Kangaroo Springs*
#3 / *Rescue at Boomerang Bend*
#4 / *Dingo Creek Challenge*
#5 / *Race to Wallaby Bay*
#6 / *Firestorm at Kookaburra Station*
#7 / *Koala Beach Outbreak*
#8 / *Panic at Emu Flat*

THE YOUNG UNDERGROUND

#1 / *A Way Through the Sea*
#2 / *Beyond the River*
#3 / *Into the Flames*
#4 / *Far From the Storm*
#5 / *Chasing the Wind*
#6 / *A Light in the Castle*
#7 / *Follow the Star*
#8 / *Touch the Sky*

ASTROKIDS

#1 / *The Great Galaxy Goof*
#2 / *The Zero-G Headache*
#3 / *Wired Wonder Woof*
#4 / *Miko's Muzzy Mess*

ROBERT ELMER

FIRESTORM AT KOOKABURRA STATION

BETHANY HOUSE PUBLISHERS
MINNEAPOLIS, MINNESOTA 55438

Firestorm at Kookaburra Station
Copyright © 1999
Robert Elmer

Cover illustration by Chris Ellison
Cover design by the Lookout Design Group

Published by Bethany House Publishers
A Ministry of Bethany Fellowship International
11400 Hampshire Avenue South
Bloomington, Minnesota 55438
www.bethanyhouse.com

Printed in the United States of America by
Bethany Press International, Bloomington, Minnesota 55438

ISBN 0–7642–2104–3

To Wayne and Adonna,
Blake, Caleb, and Andrew—
on to new adventures!

MEET ROBERT ELMER

ROBERT ELMER is the author of THE YOUNG UNDERGROUND series, as well as many magazine and newspaper articles. He lives with his wife, Ronda, and their three children, Kai, Danica, and Stefan (and their dog, Freckles), in a Washington State farming community just a bike ride away from the Canadian border.

CONTENTS

1.	Breaking Loose	11
2.	Breakaway	21
3.	The Bunyip	29
4.	Crash Landing	35
5.	Where's Mr. Graham?	41
6.	First Rescue	47
7.	Meeting the Giant	53
8.	Message in the Dust	59
9.	Accused	67
10.	Journey to Kookaburra Station	75
11.	Finding Ibby	81
12.	Runaway Brumby	89
13.	The Camel Trap	97
14.	Something in the Air	105
15.	Fighting the Firestorm	113
16.	Wall of Flames	121
17.	Unexpected Friend	127
18.	Evacuate!	133
19.	Panic at the Wharf	137
20.	River Rescue	143
21.	*Lady Elisabeth*, Lifeboat	149
22.	Lost in Wentworth	157
23.	He Meant It for Evil	163
	The Real Firestorm	169

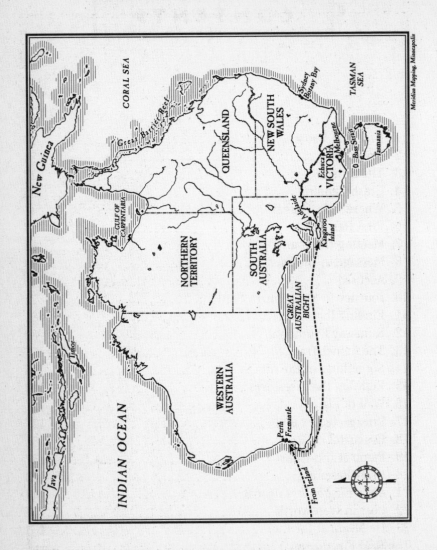

New Guinea

CORAL SEA

Great Barrier Reef

QUEENSLAND

NEW SOUTH WALES

Sydney
Botany Bay

TASMAN SEA

Melbourne

0 Bass Strait

Tasmania

VICTORIA

Echuca

GULF OF CARPENTARIA

NORTHERN TERRITORY

SOUTH AUSTRALIA

Adelaide

Kangaroo Island

Timor

Java

INDIAN OCEAN

WESTERN AUSTRALIA

GREAT AUSTRALIAN BIGHT

Perth
Fremantle

From Ireland

N
W   E
S

Meridian Mapping, Minneapolis

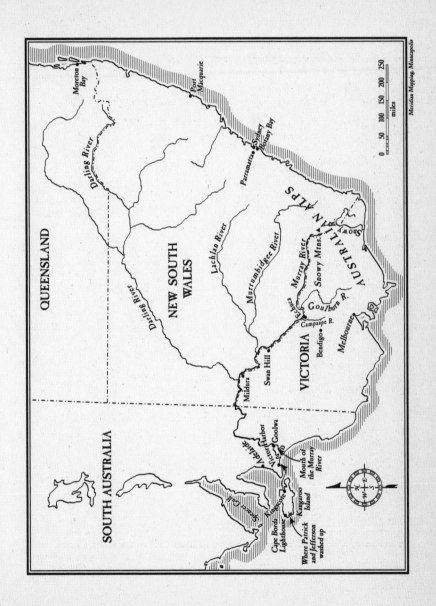

QUEENSLAND

SOUTH AUSTRALIA

NEW SOUTH WALES

VICTORIA

AUSTRALIAN ALPS

Moreton Bay

Darling River

Port Macquarie

Parramatta
Sydney
Botany Bay

Lachlan River

Darling River

Murrumbidgee River

Murray River

Snowy Mtns.

Snow

Echuca

Goulburn R.

Campaspe R.

Bendigo

Melbourne

Mildura

Swan Hill

Adelaide

Victor Harbor
Goolwa

Mouth of
the Murray
River

Spencer Gulf

Kangaroo
Island

Cape Borda
Lighthouse

Where Patrick
and Jefferson
washed up

0   50   100   150   200   250
miles

Meridian Mapping, Minneapolis

N
W   E
S

CHAPTER 1

BREAKING LOOSE

"Ahh, this is the life!"

Thirteen-year-old Patrick McWaid stared up at the clouds and listened to the churning of the paddle steamer's wheels as they plowed through the coffee-colored Murray River. Trying hard not to feel the stab of guilt, he avoided his mother and sat on the far forward deck of the *Lady Elisabeth.*

She'll find me soon enough, he told himself.

Patrick could see everything from his perch—the whitewashed steamer with a black cloud of smoke pouring from its twin funnels, the riverbanks only a stone's throw on either side, the blue-green eucalyptus trees that lined each shore, and the fluffy white clouds overhead in a wide blue afternoon sky.

And of course he could see his sister, Becky, two years older than he, standing straight backed behind the big wooden steering wheel up in the paddle steamer's wheelhouse. As her shoulder-length nut-brown hair waved in the breeze, she turned the little ship first a bit to the right, then to the left. She had to stand on a wooden box to see over the polished, wood-spoked wheel, but she was never one to let her small size hold her back.

Becky was a lot like their mother that way, with fine, delicate features and a quiet strength that helped her do lots of things Patrick didn't think most other girls could do. Still, it hadn't been easy to keep the *Lady E* afloat and on schedule—especially not on their first voyage without their grandfather.

"Are we there yet, Becky?" Patrick sat up, still keeping an eye out for his mother. With his luck she would probably come out on deck just about now looking for him.

"Not yet," Becky called back. "But you should be concentrating on finishing your chores. I'm concentrating on finding the Darling."

"Did you mean the Darling River or the darling sailor?" Patrick ignored her comment about the chores.

"You hush!" Becky was looking for the place where the Darling River joined the Murray, near the river port of Wentworth, where they would tie up for a load of wool. And just then Patrick couldn't see the "darling sailor," their friend Jefferson Pitney. Maybe he was standing back in the corner, behind Becky. He was about Becky's age and tended to spend most of his free time up in the wheelhouse, too—at least when it was Becky's turn to steer. And now that it *was* her turn to steer, it was Patrick's turn to help clean up the midday dishes.

Patrick leaned back and reached over the side of the boat to feel the cool spray on his tanned arm. January was summer in Australia, and the river was already getting low. Whoever had said 1869 would be a hot, dry year was exactly right.

But for now Patrick didn't care to think about droughts, or even about the past few months they had spent getting the paddle steamer ready for their trip up the river. Flies, sun, hard work, and plenty of it! Patrick hadn't minded the work before his grandfather died three months ago. The Old Man used to help them do everything on the boat, showed them which way to turn so they wouldn't run aground, told them his stories of the river. But now . . .

Patrick clenched his teeth. If getting mad at Grandfather for dying could bring him back . . . well, the Old Man would surely have been standing there in the flesh long ago.

Maybe if I could just get away from the work for a day or two, thought Patrick, staring down at the water and wrinkling his nose. He didn't need the mirrored river to show him his sizable collection of freckles, dusted across his cheeks like the Milky Way across the starry night sky.

"That's what happens to red-haired people like us," his father had told him once with a smile. "We suffer from those fearsome freckles."

"Fearsome," true. But "fearsome" was a better word to describe the sun lately. It had blazed on without mercy, day after day, ever since Grandfather died. Worse yet, it showed no sign of letting up. But that didn't seem to bother Becky, who didn't share Patrick's red hair or rather large ears that always seemed to get sunburned.

One thing Becky and Patrick *did* share, though, were the family's emerald green eyes, and hers sparkled in the bright late afternoon sun as she studied another twist in the river ahead. Patrick couldn't hear above the water sounds and the puffing of their steam engine, but he guessed she was probably humming another bouncy Irish tune as they followed the river's snakelike course.

"Ma's looking for you, Patrick." Another voice broke into Patrick's thoughts. "And she wants you to—"

"I know, I know," Patrick answered his eight-year-old brother, Michael, without looking. "Don't you fret about it."

Before he could feel guilty again for avoiding his chores, Patrick felt a small pair of hands start to push on his side. He pushed back.

"Don't, Michael." Patrick grabbed his brother by the arms and squeezed hard as they wrestled on the deck. Michael was smaller and rounder than his big brother, and Patrick sometimes thought he looked like an elf. Still, Michael put up a good fight as they rolled on the deck.

"It's too hot for this kind of thing," Patrick finally complained when he had Michael pinned to the deck.

"You just say that because you're losing." Michael grunted and tried to wriggle free, which of course he couldn't. He arched his back and pointed. "Patrick, do you see what's up ahead? A balloon!"

"You can't trick me. Give up."

"No, really. Look!"

Wiping the sweat from his forehead, Patrick let his brother free and looked up the river. They were nearly to Wentworth. Had to be. And in the distance something big and bright floated up in the air. The afternoon sun hit Patrick straight in the eyes.

"Hmm." Patrick squinted harder. "Maybe you're right."

"'Course I am." Michael squinted, too, and sneezed from looking into the sunshine. "Looks like a big full moon, only with colors."

"I've never seen one of those before." Patrick stared as the balloon drifted higher, by that time far above the trees. Jefferson now leaned out of the wheelhouse, too, the big American boy shading his eyes for a better view.

"Do y'all see the balloon up that way?" Jefferson—big muscled, square jawed, and powerful—sometimes sounded very much as if he had just stepped off the boat from his family's farm in Augusta, Arkansas. He looked as excited as Michael.

Balloon . . . Patrick thought for a moment what it would be like to ride above the trees, to look down on the river, to wave at everyone down on the *Lady Elisabeth*. As they came closer, they could hear people in the bustling river town of Wentworth cheering and clapping as the balloon floated up and down. A circle of flags tied around the balloon flapped in the fresh breeze.

"Faster!" Michael looked up at his sister, begging her to order more steam. "We have to go see the balloon!"

"What, you think you're going to get a ride?" Jefferson grinned.

Michael looked up at their friend with raised eyebrows. "Of course," he replied matter-of-factly.

"Oh really?" Jefferson chuckled. "I'd like to see that."

"Just watch me." Michael jumped up and down. "We just have to get there faster, that's all."

But tending the engine was up to their father, and Mr. McWaid peeked out at them from the engine room with a black-smudged face only moments before they came to a sudden, shuddering halt.

"Stuck in the mud *again*?" Michael asked, a quarter hour after they had first come to a halt.

No one answered; the answer was obvious. Patrick was now used to the shifting shallows that made navigating the Murray River such a challenge—and such a bother sometimes.

"I still think it's interesting," mused Becky, watching the river, "how the two colors of the two rivers run side by side. Cream on one side from the Darling River and—"

"Coffee on the other side from the Murray," interrupted Michael, dipping his foot down into the water. Becky pulled him back up.

"A little less chatting, please," snapped their father as he hurried by. "See what you can do to make yourself useful."

"Why is he so serious?" Patrick looked to Jefferson with his question as soon as his father had returned to the engine room.

"Don't you know?" asked Jefferson, the sweat standing out on his forehead. "We've been promised a prime load of wool. It's supposed to be waiting for us in Wentworth. But if we don't get there in time, someone else will probably get it instead."

The older boy coiled the heavy anchor chain around the sideways-facing metal drum on the front deck. A long handle on the side of the winch let them crank in the chain and drag themselves over the mud one inch at a time.

"Even if it's promised to us?" Patrick helped crank the chain. Jefferson shrugged.

"But that wouldn't be fair," added Michael.

Jefferson sighed. "Fair or not, you can figure it for yourself. Your pa is making payments on that new boiler for the engine, right? No money from the wool means no money for the payment. No money for the payment, and the bank's got every right to take back their boiler. Or maybe even the boat."

Patrick shook his head, remembering how they had already almost lost the *Lady Elisabeth* before his grandfather died. He still had dreams once in a while about steering the *Lady E* and hitting a log. Dreams where the wheel would not turn and the boat would not move. Patrick shuddered.

That's not going to happen again, Patrick promised himself. He tried not to think of what it had been like when Grandfather was in command of the paddle steamer. Since the funeral Patrick had already cried more than he wanted to.

Not now. He commanded his watery eyes to stop. *Not again*.

"Helloo!" called a deckhand on a passing paddle steamer. "Forgot to bring your river chart with you, eh, mate?" Patrick read the name on the proud, newly painted wheelhouse: the *Adelaide*.

"We're doing just fine!" shouted Patrick, feeling the heat in the back of his neck as he made a face at the *Adelaide*. "So why don't you—"

"Patrick, hush," scolded his sister. "You watch your Irish temper."

"Grandfather would never have let us run aground." Patrick kicked hard at a rope on the deck but missed, kicking a sharp metal cleat instead.

"Ow!" he cried, hopping on one foot.

"See what happens?" said Becky. His face red, Patrick turned away from the laughing men on the other paddle steamer. His toe throbbed.

Actually, the waves from the passing paddle steamer helped a bit; when they hit, Jefferson was all set to crank even harder as they hopped off the mud for an instant. The *Lady E* jerked and heaved as if she were having a coughing fit. Even with the lurching and Jefferson's frantic cranking, though, Patrick figured they weren't going anywhere very soon.

"Looks like we'll be spending the rest of the day on the river," admitted Patrick with a sigh. The paddle wheels churned furiously.

"It's not fair," Michael whined as he crossed his arms and squinted at the sun sinking lower behind the big balloon. "Maybe we should just swim over to the town."

They *were* pretty close. But Patrick and the others had to settle for a back-row seat as they watched the big balloon rise up in the warm afternoon air, tug on the end of its long leash, then slowly drop down again. Another hour passed, and Patrick worried that each craft coming up the river would steal their wool.

Over on shore, the people cheered as they watched the riders— one or two at a time—take to the sky. The third person in the balloon's basket was obviously piloting the craft. Even from a distance Patrick could make out the man's tall black stovepipe hat—the same kind the recent American president Lincoln had always worn.

"Fella's gonna lose his big hat," Jefferson grunted as he took another turn on the anchor chain.

Yet another passing paddle steamer hurried by, black smoke billowing from its stacks and a deafening whistle echoing up and down the river. It tipped slightly to the right as a lineup of passengers leaned over the side railing to wave and point.

"Weekenders!" Jeff spit out the word under his breath. "Actin' like they've never laid eyes on a real working paddle steamer before."

Patrick held on as the wave from the passing paddle steamer washed their way. At least it wasn't a competing cargo boat.

"Hold on, boys!" Becky called down from the wheelhouse, but the wave had already hit. This time they were lifted up and forward. Jefferson cranked the anchor chain as if his life depended on it while Patrick stooped to keep the muddy chain from getting tangled.

"Watch your hand," warned Mr. McWaid just as a link in the chain twisted and nipped Patrick's fingers.

"Ow!" Patrick yanked his hand back in pain, but he didn't have time to worry about it. The *Lady Elisabeth* rocked and swayed.

"We're free!" Michael peeked over the edge of the weathered wooden deck to see the river rush by. "Aren't we?"

It was true. Even Mrs. McWaid came out to see.

"Well, well." She smiled and held on to the back of Michael's shirt so he wouldn't lean too far. "Maybe we should be thanking the weekenders for floating us off that mudbank. And you, Patrick, you're quite good at chores when you've a mind to be."

"Yes, Ma," answered Patrick, doing his best to avoid his mother's look.

Jefferson cranked in the remaining anchor chain while Patrick and Michael tugged the anchor into place on the forward deck.

"Now we'll get to see the balloon after all." Michael danced a jig as they neared the Wentworth wharf. They would pull into place behind the other two paddle steamers that had passed them.

"First the wool," Mr. McWaid reminded them. "No one leaves until we've loaded our share."

Patrick nodded as he watched the fascinating show. They could hear the crowd "ooh" and "ahh" as another passenger took to the sky in the wicker basket. Hanging below and flapping in the wind, a jaunty white banner with sewn-on red letters proclaimed

J. P. Graham, Esq., Astounding Aerial Excursions

"What does e–s–q spell, Patrick?" Michael wanted to know.

"It's short for esquire. That's a fancy name for—"

"For somebody who wants to be called by a fancy name," put in Jefferson.

Patrick smiled and nodded. "Something like that. Thank you."

Back in the esquire's balloon, the passenger was taking no chances. An older woman had latched on to the man in the black stovepipe hat and looked as if she wasn't ever going to let loose. At least not before the balloon made it back down to the ground. He looked as if he was trying to convince her to enjoy the view, but she was obviously not going to be convinced.

"I'm going to ride in that balloon," announced Michael.

"No, you're not," Patrick snapped in his best big-brother voice. "So stop talking about something you can't do. Besides, it's dangerous. See how the wind is picking them up and pushing them around?"

"I don't care. And you don't have to be so cross." Michael crossed his arms, set his jaw, and rocked up on his toes for a better view. True, the afternoon breeze was punching the balloon and its basket around like a little toy. But obviously that only made it seem more interesting to Michael.

"You have to pay for a ride, you know," said Jefferson, with a grin at the others. Now, *there* was an obstacle. Michael's face fell, and he looked back over his shoulder at the older boy.

"How do you know?"

"Says right there on the sign, see? 'Rides, ten shillings.' "

Michael bobbed as he studied the balloon again. "Well, doesn't matter. I'll figure a way."

Not if I can help it, thought Patrick, almost wishing he could tie his brother down, just like the balloon.

CHAPTER 2

BREAKAWAY

Patrick knew better than to let Michael out of his sight. But for the rest of the afternoon, Patrick's younger brother didn't have a chance to get into trouble—not with all the chores they needed to finish. This time there was no escaping them.

"Those supplies there." Mr. McWaid pointed at a pile of wooden crates that still needed unloading before they could load up a wool barge. He didn't need to say it twice. Though he wasn't extremely big, their red-bearded father was obviously in command. He would look at something with his sparkling hazel eyes, grin, and nod, and Patrick knew what to do.

And after having been on the river a few weeks, Becky, Michael, and Jefferson knew the routine, too. Tie up at another stop, make sure the paddle steamer wouldn't wander or bang against the wharf or any other boats, help with the loading and unloading. Splitting and loading firewood for the steam engine was the worst. But normally once all those chores were done, they were free to explore. And Wentworth looked a lot more interesting than some of the little bark cabins they had seen along the way.

"But what about the wool?" asked Patrick, scanning the empty wharf. "Did someone take it already?"

Most of the dock workers had by that time hurried home for supper, or else they had drifted over to the crowd of townspeople that had circled J. P. Graham's big balloon.

Mr. McWaid shook his head. "The wool's late, the agent on the wharf tells me. But nobody seems to know why it hasn't arrived from the station."

"See?" Mrs. McWaid smiled at them. "All that worry for nothing."

But Jefferson wasn't convinced. "Something's not right. I've a good mind to go see for myself what's holding it up."

By that time Patrick knew there would be no more chores until morning—and that was good news.

After getting directions, Jefferson left for the sheep station to find out about the missing wool. And after dinner, Becky, Patrick, and Michael went ashore to explore Wentworth.

"Where *is* that Michael?" wondered Becky, searching the empty wharf for her youngest brother, who was suddenly nowhere to be seen. The wharf was a bit smaller than the one they were used to in Echuca, farther upriver. And the bank of the river was gentler here, too—not as steep as it was in the river town they had called home.

"I think I know." Patrick mopped his forehead in the heat and jerked his thumb in the direction of the balloon.

"We'd better go see what he's doing before it gets dark." Becky bounded across the wharf toward town.

Look away for one moment, fumed Patrick, *and he's gone*.

As they hurried across the dusty street to a field behind a crooked storefront, Patrick imagined Michael high up in the balloon, looking down at them. Patrick arrived to find nearly a hundred people crowded around the grounded balloon.

At least it's not up in the air right now.

The balloon itself looked more than ready to go, tugging at its ropes like a frisky pony on a leash. Patrick had to stop and stare.

"I've never seen such a sight," whispered Becky, her eyes wide.

"I hadn't imagined it would be so big, either."

Without another word, they just stood together for a few minutes watching. For a moment Patrick almost forgot why they had come.

"I'm terribly sorry, good ladies and gentlemen of Wentworth." The man in the stovepipe hat finally lifted his hands in apology. "The winds are a trifle fresh, and as much as I would like to accommodate you, we'd best cease operations for the day. After all, it *will* be getting dark soon."

The pudgy, pink-faced man wore a wrinkled black suit that looked unbearably hot to Patrick. His large cheeks seemed to flap in the wind.

"I don't see him." Becky was still scanning the crowd. Patrick couldn't see Michael, either—not until Becky pointed at a pair of little feet disappearing into the back of the wicker basket. The balloonist was too busy talking with his crowd to notice.

"Oh no!" Patrick slipped through the people to catch his brother. *Maybe we can get him out of there quietly.*

Becky must have had the same thought as she reached up to grab the rim of the basket. But she wasn't as lucky as Michael had been. Or maybe *lucky* wasn't the right word.

"Say, there, young lady!" J. P. Graham noticed them out of the corner of his eye. "You'll need to back away."

"But my little brother—"

"Your little brother will have to wait until tomorrow morning, just like everyone else. Now, run along, please. The wind is too brisk."

Then, as if to prove his point, the wind gusted.

"The ropes!" someone yelled as one of the three safety ropes that held the balloon to the ground whistled by Patrick's head. A woman screamed, and the crowd backed away as the basket lurched.

"It's all right. Not to worry!" J. P. Graham put up his hands and tried to calm them down. But now the balloon and its basket were swinging wildly through the crowd, scattering people like a flock of frightened sea gulls. Patrick watched helplessly as the basket bumped into an older boy and sent him flying. It almost would have been funny, except . . .

Michael finally peeked over the edge of the balloon, his eyes as big as saucers.

"Michael!" cried Patrick. The wind wasn't letting up, and the single stake holding the last rope to the ground was wiggling like a loose tooth. Michael's lips moved, but no sound came out. Becky tried to pick herself off the ground, but the basket swung back over her and she ducked back down. Only J. P. Graham stood statue-still, his face beet red. The man pointed a quivering finger at the out-of-control basket.

"You get out of there!" he demanded, but he might as well have told the wind to be still. Michael ducked down as the wild basket plowed over another row of people.

We have to rescue him, thought Patrick, but he could only dodge the two loose ropes that shot over their heads. A mother next to him pulled her daughter to the ground.

"I said," began the balloonist once more, in his most commanding voice, "get out of that basket IMMEDIATELY!"

"I'm sorry!" squeaked Michael as the basket swung directly down at J. P. Graham like a giant pendulum.

Instead of falling over on his back, though, the balloonist grabbed a handhold and flipped over the edge of the basket, head over heels, landing with a grunt next to Michael.

The last rope pulled free, spraying dirt all over Patrick's head. He put his hand up to keep the dirt out of his eyes, but as he did, he felt the rope wrap around his right arm like a snake. Patrick yelped in pain as it nearly yanked his arm out of its socket. He leaped—or rather, was yanked to his feet.

The big, round monster began to pitch and bump along the ground and through the bushes like a multicolored tumbleweed. Michael hollered and would have jumped, but J. P. Graham held him down.

Patrick, meanwhile, was the balloon's new anchor—though not a very good one. He stumbled along behind the balloon, half dragging, half running, trying to stay on his feet. The rope burned his forearm. It was no longer tangled, but Patrick had locked his grip on the loose safety line.

"Let go, Patrick," Michael yelled from the edge of the basket.

"Not with you up there," Patrick replied through his gritted teeth. Still the balloon bumped along, not sure if it wanted to fly or tumble. A lone tree up ahead stood in the way.

Maybe I could loop the rope around a branch, Patrick thought. It would be his last chance to do something. It was either that or let go and watch his brother disappear into the dark evening sky.

"That tree!" Patrick tried to yell at the two in the balloon. J. P. Graham turned around for a moment and seemed to understand. He waved wildly at Patrick.

"Let go, lad!" was all Patrick could hear over the sound of the wind and the whipping of the bushes. That wasn't what Patrick had in mind.

A sandbag dropped off beside him, then another. The balloonist was ready to let loose another to lighten the load when Patrick felt the ground drop away below his feet. He pumped his legs as if he were still running to keep up with the escaping balloon, but nothing was there. Nothing except the tree branches as they scraped by. With a flash of pink wings and a loud screech, a galah parrot scolded them and headed for another perch.

"You have to let go, Patrick!" Michael's eyes were wide and his face pale as he looked down at his brother. "I mean, hold on!"

As he swung on the end of the rope, this time hanging on to the sturdy wooden stake like a swing, Patrick guessed he knew what a circus trapeze artist must feel like. He looked down once—only once—and that was enough to remind him that he was a long way from the circus.

Judging from the size of the people on the ground, he would soon be a long way from anything. *Oh, my stomach*. The thought crossed his mind just for an instant that he might be sick, but there was no time to think about it. He inched his way up the rope, hand over hand, hoping to grasp the rim of the basket and pull himself over the edge.

A few minutes later Patrick lay on his back in the bottom of the four-foot-square basket, gasping and shaking and not at all sure what he was doing in such a strange place. Better here, though, than hanging by a thin rope. Michael kneeled down next to him.

"You all right, Patrick?"

"Give me a minute." Patrick tried to catch his breath from climbing up the rope. "I'll let you know."

"Give him some air," barked the balloonist as he replaced the stovepipe hat on his head.

"Aye," agreed Patrick, rubbing the rope burn on his wrists. "A little air would be good."

When Michael helped his older brother to his feet, Patrick quickly changed his mind. Suddenly there was plenty of air all around them, stretching as far as he could see. He gripped his stomach and closed his eyes as the basket creaked from their weight and swung briskly in the breeze.

"What happened to the wind?" asked Michael. Patrick, too, had noticed that the whirlwind had calmed down a bit.

J. P. Graham gave a smile for the first time since the balloon had broken loose, a smile framed by his enormous cheeks. Then he licked the end of his finger and held it up.

"What happened to the wind? Why, it's still there, of course. Pretty healthy breeze, at that. Only now we're traveling with it instead of against it. But you two . . ."

His voice turned serious, and his face turned red as he began to scold them for the fix they were in.

"You two have no right to cause this kind of trouble. No right at all. Why, if we weren't so high up right now, I'd . . . I'd . . ."

His voice trailed off as he looked around at the view. Patrick took a deep breath and looked, too. Far below, the chocolate brown Murray River snaked through the beautiful but flat Riverina country on its way to the sea. From this height he could see clearly where the *Lady Elisabeth* had gone aground, and he traced their route up through the double band of eucalyptus trees that hugged the banks on either side of the river. But in the distance the sky was darkening.

Beyond that the dry grasslands seemed to curve off into the distance forever, beautiful and lonely, until they met the horizon, where the orange sun had already set. Even with the butterflies in his stomach and the lump in his throat, it was enough to take Patrick's breath away.

"What did you think you were doing in this balloon?" J. P. Graham asked his youngest passenger. Michael shrank away, almost hiding behind Patrick.

"Please, sir, I'm sorry. I just thought that if I was in the basket, you might take me up with the next riders."

"And I suppose you'll be telling me you didn't have the money for a ride, eh?" The balloonist had obviously heard the story before.

Michael nodded. "Yes, sir. I'm sorry, sir. I'll pay you back somehow."

J. P. Graham shook his head. "I suppose I should be upset. But look here. One day everyone will be able to fly about the world like this. You are seeing the future, lads. Have you ever seen a view so grand?"

Patrick had not, and he had even started to relax his grip on the edge of the basket. The deep, dark colors! From yellow to gold, to pink and orange, finally to a deep red that filled the sky. No, he had never seen anything so grand in all his life.

"Have you been up this high before?" wondered Michael. The balloonist frowned.

"Certainly. After all, I *am* J. P. Graham. But I must say, we've caught quite a draft. We're moving up faster than a galloping horse."

Michael and Patrick both nodded, as if they knew how famous and important J. P. Graham was supposed to be. Patrick then caught his stomach as the balloon suddenly dipped and swayed.

"It's dropping!" Patrick hollered. It seemed his stomach remained somewhere above his head. He gripped the basket railing and thought for an instant what his parents and Becky would do when they found the wreck of the balloon.

CHAPTER 3

THE BUNYIP

"Come, now, you're not going to panic each time we hit a small patch of rough air, are you?" J. P. Graham adjusted a sandbag as Patrick tried to find his stomach again. Michael was smiling as if he was having the time of his life.

"Do you go flying like this, off your leash, all the time?" asked Michael.

J. P. Graham surveyed his world and breathed deeply. "My 'leash'? Oh, you mean the safety line your brother climbed up? Why, certainly. There was the World's Fair in Paris last year, and London, of course. Crowds love me wherever I go, you see."

"I see." Patrick nodded.

Michael squinted toward the dark landscape, watching a bank of even darker clouds on the horizon.

"What are those clouds?" he asked. "Does that mean it's going to rain?"

Patrick looked more closely. His father would be happy to hear about the clouds. So would everybody around there. It hadn't rained in months on the thirsty land below them.

"And then there was the time in Rome when I would have set a European distance record." J. P. Graham ignored them as he rattled on. "Only the wind picked up from the wrong direction, just like today. It wasn't my fault, you see."

Patrick kept his eyes on the clouds. "Looks like rain to me," he told his brother.

"Hmm. Looks like night to me." Michael tried spitting over the edge to see what would happen. They both watched as long as they could, but they were up too high and the spit faded from view. Patrick thought he could see horses following them, but Mr. Graham was right about how fast they were going. As the balloonist kept bragging about how far he had traveled in a balloon and how much the world adored him, Patrick watched as the dark bank of clouds to the west seemed to grow taller and taller. By then the river and the town of Wentworth were far behind in the dark shadows. A flash of light from the clouds caught his attention.

"Did you see that?" asked Michael.

"Lightning." Patrick nodded and shivered in the cooler evening air.

"Eh?" The balloonist finally turned to see what they were watching. "Clouds? Lightning? Why didn't you say so?"

Patrick pointed at the next flash of lightning, still far off in the distance. They couldn't even hear any thunder, it was so far away.

"Oh, it's that dust storm people have been talking about." Mr. Graham squinted at the clouds. "Nothing to fret over. I've been through much worse. Why, there was the time in Zanzibar when a Zulu warrior came up to the balloon, or perhaps that was Kenya. . . ."

The stories went on like that for a while, and Patrick watched the dark land far below their feet. Was it a thousand feet below? Ten thousand? Once in a while he saw birds, even the shadowy shape of a kangaroo family hopping across the fields. Everything looked like tiny toys. But something kept him from enjoying the view.

"Ah, excuse me, sir," said Patrick.

The man frowned. He had just reached the part of his story where tigers were stalking him, ready to pounce.

"Uh . . . I was just wondering how far we were going to go. I mean, our parents will be wondering what happened to us."

"Your *parents*?" asked the balloonist. The way he turned up his nose and wrinkled his forehead made Patrick believe the thought had never crossed his mind.

"Our mother and father." Patrick pointed down at the ground with his thumb. "It's been a while since we took off. I'm sure our sister told them what happened and—"

"And they'll follow, if it's a concern to them," interrupted the balloonist.

"But how far have we gone?" wondered Michael.

"Who knows?" answered Mr. Graham. "But of course I'm quite well known for my perfect safety record, so you needn't worry."

"Of course." Patrick crossed his arms. "But *my parents* are still going to be worried."

"Trifles and details." He sniffed at them. "I can see you're not yet understanding the future of the human race, my boys. It's not down there on the dismal plains of earth. Not among the earth-bound mortals. The future is up *here*, I say. In the air! Can't you feel it? Don't you see?"

Patrick nodded. "I see. But don't you think we'd better get down to the dismal plains before it's too dark?"

"Young people these days have no patience to see the future," complained Mr. Graham. He reached high over his head and pulled gently on a cord to let out some of the gas through the top of the balloon. At first it stuck, then he tugged a little harder, and they heard a *whoosh*. Patrick felt a slight jolt as they headed down, and Michael grabbed Patrick's arm.

"Look down there!" Michael pointed at a shadowy grove of short trees clustered around the glitter of a small water hole, one of the few they had seen in the parched landscape. "See the water?"

"Is that what it is?" Patrick squinted to make sure. "With our luck we'll land in the only water for miles."

"No, not the water hole." Michael took Patrick's chin in his hand and tried to make him see what he had seen. "A lantern over there, just through the trees. That way. See?"

It took a moment, but Patrick's eyes locked on to a flicker of yellow light moving in the bush. An animal moved not far from that. It wasn't a kangaroo or a man, but something bigger. Much bigger.

"I can't really make it out." Patrick strained to see better. "Too dark. You think it's a horse?"

Michael shook his head. "Looks bigger than a horse."

Patrick could see his brother was right, but it seemed strange. In the Australian outback, no animal was bigger than a horse. And from what they could see, this thing had an odd, long neck. Mr. Graham laughed without even looking down.

"You've sighted a bunyip, have you?"

"Say that again?" Patrick wasn't sure he'd heard right.

"Bunyip. That's what the aborigines call it." This time the performer had his audience's attention as they dropped closer and closer to the ground. If they kept the way they were going, they would touch down a few hundred feet beyond the trees where Michael had spotted the creature. But Patrick couldn't see it anymore.

"Is it some kind of animal?" asked Michael.

Mr. Graham shook his head. "Not entirely. The native story goes that the bunyip is half beast, half man. A huge, hairy creature with a long neck and the head of either a horse or a bird. Eyes big as your fist. Big ears that flap like so." Mr. Graham acted out the part of the bunyip, widening his eyes and putting his hands up to the top of his head like ears.

"They live in swamps, billabongs, and such," he continued, obviously enjoying the story. "But I wouldn't worry yourself. The aborigines have plenty of legends like that. The only thing I'd worry about is if I heard the bunyip's scream. *That's* how you can tell a bunyip, even if you don't see it."

"The *scream*?" Michael wanted to know more.

"As I said, not to worry. It's a bloodcurdling cry. You'd know it if you heard it."

Patrick rolled his eyes at the silly story and watched the shadows on the ground as they dropped lower and lower. The evening cast a deep silence on the Australian countryside. And then he heard it.

"What was that?" Michael nearly jumped into Patrick's arms.

"Let go of me," Patrick told his brother. "It was just an animal."

But the hair on the back of his neck stood on end, and he leaned over to hear better, wishing they were a little higher and going up instead of a little lower and going down. And there it was again: a grunt, a wheeze, a frightened kind of scream.

"There!" Michael didn't let go of Patrick's arm this time.

"I heard it, too." Patrick tried to keep his teeth from chattering. The air *was* kind of cool by now, after all. "It was coming from right down below us."

Patrick looked over the edge at the land as it grew closer and closer. And for the first time J. P. Graham seemed worried. Quickly, he emptied the last of the sand out of his bags, but still they dropped like a stone out of the sky.

"You'd better hold on," he told them quietly. Even in the cool air, Patrick noticed sweat on the man's forehead. "It seems I've miscalculated slightly."

"But you've done this lots of times before, haven't you?" questioned Patrick. "What about all the trips you've made to Paris and Rome and London?"

Mr. Graham didn't answer right away. When Patrick looked up at him, the balloonist looked a bit pale.

"Well . . ." Mr. Graham pulled at his starched collar. "I have to admit that conditions there weren't quite so . . . primitive."

Patrick wasn't sure what their pilot meant, but suddenly the ground didn't look very far away at all.

"We're falling!" cried Michael.

"Depends on how you look at things," replied the pilot through clenched teeth. "But just remember, all it takes is good looks and a little cleverness to overcome any problem, I always say."

Patrick peeked over the edge as the ground rushed to meet them. He squeezed his eyes shut, held on to his brother with one hand, bent his legs, and gripped the edge of the basket with the other hand. Michael said nothing.

"This could be a trifle bumpy, boys."

CHAPTER 4

CRASH LANDING

J. P. Graham has a way with words, thought Patrick as the basket hit the ground hard once and bounced away. Their pilot grunted and lost his footing as they turned sideways and dragged across the scrubland.

"Patrick!" Michael called out in fright. It was all Patrick could do to hold on to his brother. And surely the landing was much worse than even their bumpy takeoff. They tumbled over and around, and they heard J. P. Graham's cry as he flew from the basket.

"We lost him!" Patrick cried out.

Still the basket tumbled, dragged by the wind and the canopy of the balloon still over them, smashing through bushes and trees. Patrick tried to cover them both with his arm to keep from being thrown out the way Mr. Graham had been. Branches lashed out at them, they hit a rock, and then finally their wild ride slowed. Patrick looked to the side so he could breathe in spite of Michael's grip around his neck. Another rock. Another tree, but this one only bent slowly, and then there was silence.

"Where are we, Patrick?" Michael was the first to say anything.

"If you can get your head out of my back, I'll be able to tell."

The boys untangled themselves from each other and fell to the wet ground.

"Ooh," said Michael. "This is muddy. And why—"

"I think we're upside-down under the basket," explained Patrick. "Are you all right?"

"I think so."

Patrick felt his arms and wiggled his legs to make sure everything was working the way it should.

At least we didn't break any bones, he thought. Under his knees, though, he could feel something oozing between his fingers. Even more than that, he could smell the rich mud of the water hole they had seen from the air. He tried to straighten out but bumped his head on the bottom of the basket.

"Give me a hand, Michael, and we'll get out from underneath this thing. Remember, all we need is good looks and a little cleverness—"

"You don't believe that, do you?"

"Of course not. I was just trying to make you feel better."

"Where's Mr. Graham?" The quiver in Michael's voice told Patrick his brother was about to cry.

"Don't worry." Patrick tried to sound like his father. "He fell out as soon as we hit the ground. He's probably out looking for us. All we have to do is yell and—"

Patrick was interrupted by the grunting, screaming sound they had heard from the air.

"There it is again." Michael grabbed at his brother as if he were drowning. "You don't think Mr. Graham was right, do you? About the bunyip?"

"Don't be silly." Patrick reached up to see if he could lift or tip the basket over. "We're getting out of here."

But the basket was heavier than Patrick had thought, and Michael launched into a storm of tears.

"It's all my fault," blubbered Michael. "If I had stayed out of the basket, we wouldn't be here."

"We had a good ride, though, didn't we?" Patrick tried to settle him down. "We're not that far from Wentworth. We'll be all right."

"I wasn't trying to get in trouble. I just thought I could see what it looked like. But then the wind blew us so far, and now Mr. Graham is gone."

What would Pa do? Patrick wondered. He felt his brother shivering in the cool, muddy-smelling shelter, and he sighed.

"All right, where's your hand?" Patrick finally said, reaching out in the darkness. After a moment of groping, he found Michael's shivering little hand. "We're going to pray."

"You." Michael sniffled. His voice sounded very, very small, but it echoed inside their basket hideout. Patrick took a deep breath and began.

"Lord, thank you for not letting us get hurt. Help us not to be scared at silly things. And we need to find Mr. Graham. . . ."

"But not the bunyip," added Michael.

Patrick paused and sighed. "Amen."

"Amen." Michael's voice was still quivering, but at least he wasn't bawling anymore.

That's better, thought Patrick. *Now, if we can just lift this basket out of the way—*

He jumped when something soft and wet brushed against his arm. Something alive but cold and clammy.

"Yow!" cried Patrick. He bumped his head hard on the basket floor and lifted his arms over his head like a weight lifter. It was too heavy.

"Get out, Michael!"

Patrick finally managed to tip the basket over just a little.

"Did you feel that frog?" asked Michael.

Patrick almost started to laugh. *A frog!*

Michael managed to scramble outside. Patrick could see his brother's foot disappear in the dim, reddish light from outside. Anything was lighter than the darkness under the basket.

"All right, now hold it up while I get out," Patrick commanded his brother. "Can you do that?"

"I don't know."

"Don't start your crying again. Just hold it up until I get out."

"But, Patrick—"

Patrick didn't wait for his brother to answer; he squirmed out on his stomach through the cool, squishy mud to the outside.

"I can't hold it anymore, Patrick." Michael sounded desperate. He let it go a second after Patrick pulled his legs to safety.

"That's all right." Patrick lay on his back for a moment, panting. "I didn't need my legs anyway."

Michael obviously wasn't in a joking mood.

Neither am I, for that matter, thought Patrick as he looked around. As far as he could tell, they had landed in a thicket of short, brambly trees at the edge of a muddy water hole. But it was almost too dark to tell anything. The frogs were silent, the bunyip wasn't saying anything for the moment, and the big, flat balloon stretched away on the other side of the basket, flapping in the breeze. The wind wasn't quite as gusty as it had been when they took off, but it was still strong enough to send a chill through his bones.

A sliver of a moon was coming up over the horizon, hardly enough to give them any light. And where was Mr. Graham?

"We need to yell," began Patrick, taking a deep breath.

"Shh!" insisted Michael. "The bunyip . . ."

Patrick sighed and tried to wipe the mud off his clothes as best he could. "Oh, all right. But let's at least start walking toward the moon. That's the way we came from."

"What time do you think it is?"

"I don't know. Past your bedtime."

As they walked, Patrick could just make out where they had crashed and dragged their balloon across the bog. He saw the broken branches of a short tree, not much taller than they were, and the dirt was dug up in places like giant footprints.

"Look at that, Patrick." Michael knelt down in the dirt and put his hand in one of the tracks.

"I know. It's where we dragged the basket as we were coming down."

"No, it's not. It's something different."

Patrick paused to bend down. Michael guided his hand to the spot in the soft ground. It was big and round, like a footprint, but bigger.

"Animal footprint?" Patrick wondered aloud, but he knew it was like no animal footprint he had ever seen. Though he was still wet and muddy, he tried not to shiver again.

"Let's keep going," he told Michael.

"There are a lot of those tracks around here," Michael replied, his voice quiet and steady this time. "They're from the—"

"Don't say it," Patrick cut in. "You're only making yourself more scared. It's probably just a friendly kind of animal, maybe as scared as we are."

"Y-you think so?"

"Of course. And besides, we haven't heard that sound again, have we? Whatever it was must be gone now."

Michael didn't answer, and Patrick shivered as he felt his way through the bush a foot at a time. *Where is Mr. Graham?*

"Listen, now, we must find Mr. Graham." Patrick felt the bush ahead of him. "And he must be close by."

"What if he got up and walked away without us?" worried Michael.

"What, and leave his balloon behind? I don't think so."

The only thing that worried Patrick now was whether Mr. Graham was even able to get up and walk. What if he were—

Patrick didn't let himself think about the worst that could happen. He just kept on searching the bushes, whispering louder and louder.

"Mr. Graham," he whispered, and this time Michael didn't even tell him to be quiet. "Mr. Graham, are you there?"

For a moment he thought he heard a groan. They both froze. Finally he took a baby step toward the sound.

"Mr. Graham?"

Another groan, this time a little louder.

"I think it's him," Patrick whispered to Michael, and he didn't let go of his brother's arm.

"I think it's the bunyip!" Michael whispered back, and he dug in his heels.

"Stop it, Michael." But Patrick jumped all the same when a twig snapped in front of them. His teeth started to chatter, but he was sweating at the same time.

"Mr. Graham?" Patrick took another step and tumbled over a dark shape.

CHAPTER 5

WHERE'S MR. GRAHAM?

"Ohh!" cried Patrick, and he rolled away as quickly as he could. Michael hollered in fright, but Patrick kept him from running by grabbing his ankle.

"Let go of me, Patrick!" cried Michael. "It's a dead body!"

"It is *not* a dead body," insisted Patrick, though he wasn't sure himself. "It's Mr. Graham, and he's quite alive." *Isn't he?*

"There, now!" said the body, and Patrick could barely make out the pale face of J. P. Graham. The man's eyelids fluttered in the dim light; the voice sounded confused. "Here I am dazed and barely alive, and you're trampling me in the darkness!"

"Mr. Graham," whispered Patrick, leaning as close as he dared. "It's us, Patrick and Michael. You fell out of the balloon basket."

"I did?" The dark shape held his head and sat up straight. "I don't seem to recall."

"So you're not hurt?" Patrick wanted to know.

"We've been looking for you," explained Michael, not giving Mr. Graham a chance to answer. "We were afraid you were—"

"Yes, yes, it appears you found me well enough. Now, what did you do to my balloon?"

"Your balloon's fine, I think, sir." Patrick pointed back toward where they had crash-landed. "It's just over there a ways, all laid out on the ground. But what about you? Are you sure you're all right?"

"Am I sure I'm all right? he asks. Every bone in my body is broken, and he asks if I'm all right? My expensive balloon is probably ruined, my lucky hat has disappeared, and he asks if I'm all right. I say, what does it look like, boy?"

"It looks like you're dead," whispered Michael.

"And I'll tell you something—that's exactly how it feels."

"But your hat's not missing. Here." Michael picked up Mr. Graham's stovepipe hat and Patrick tried to help the man stand, but Mr. Graham shrieked in pain and pushed him away.

"Oh, my shoulder!" he cried. "Can't you see I'm in pain? I mustn't be moved. Oh my, oh my. I'm near death, no doubt. I've heard about what happens to people in battle. Probably my shoulder is broken. And there's a very good chance I shall not live to see the morning light."

"Maybe he *did* break something," Patrick whispered to Michael. He touched Mr. Graham's shoulder gently, but the man jumped beneath his touch and yelped once more.

"Leave me alone!" he shrieked. "You hooligans nearly steal my balloon, force me to crash-land in this forsaken wilderness, and now you think you can play doctor on me! Oh, you're going to pay for this. . . ."

"Now, wait a minute—" Patrick felt the back of his neck heat up.

"Maybe we should try to start a fire," interrupted Michael. "It would warm him up and . . . keep the wild animals away."

"A fire, did you say?" asked Mr. Graham. "That's right, light a funeral pyre, a bonfire to celebrate my last moments on the earth. By all means. Perhaps someone will see it and come to your rescue. But for me, of course, it's too late."

Patrick shook his head in the darkness. "We don't have anything to start a fire with, Michael," he whispered to his brother. "All we can do is wait for the morning and pray that someone will find us."

Patrick was interrupted once more by the horrible bunyip

sound, a groaning, grunting cry that seemed to come from every-where at once. Michael jumped.

"Just an animal of some sort, I'm sure." Patrick's hand started to shake, but he pushed the picture of a big, hairy creature out of his mind and gripped his brother even harder.

"D-do you really think so?" Michael's teeth chattered.

"All right, now, listen." Patrick pulled Michael aside. "Here's what we're going to do."

Michael swallowed hard but waited.

"We're not far from town."

"How far, Patrick?"

"I figure five or six miles at most. And they must be out looking for us. I could find a house. I saw a few from the air. There are some sheep stations out here."

"No!" Michael couldn't stop shaking. "I'm going with you! You're not going to leave me here alone."

"All right, all right. I was just considering how we should best do this."

"That's all very good," the balloonist whined. "But what about me? I'm gravely injured, don't forget."

Patrick sighed, let go of his brother, and continued.

"All right, I'll stay here. But, Michael, you've got to promise *me* you won't go running off or anything if we hear that animal again. All right, Michael?"

Michael sniffled.

"Do you promise?" Patrick tried once more.

"I promise." But Michael's voice caught on a sob. Patrick crouched with his arm around his brother's shoulder. If rescuers didn't come soon, it would be a long night.

There was, of course, no way to sleep, especially not in their wet, muddy clothes. Every once in a while Michael sniffled and sighed, telling Patrick that he wasn't sleeping, either.

"Ma and Pa are out looking for us right now," whispered Michael. "Aren't they?"

"Of course they are."

But Patrick stared up at the stars, wondering.

What would Grandpa have done? he asked himself. *Looked up at the stars and steered us home? I miss him.*

Patrick dropped off a time or two, only to wake with a start, afraid he had heard the animal. But it was Mr. Graham's snoring. He sounded more content than Patrick thought he had a right to sound. And as the minutes turned to hours, Patrick wanted to plug his ears the way he shut his eyes and wish his way back to the gentle rocking safety of the *Lady Elisabeth.*

Is it morning yet? For just a moment he wondered what would happen if he and Michael quietly crawled off and walked home.

We could do it easily. It's not far.

And it wasn't. If they could just figure out the right direction to walk, they could be back to the river in a few hours. They would be home before daybreak.

Mr. Graham wouldn't miss us anyway.

But then Mr. Graham whimpered in the dark, kind of like a new puppy, and Patrick knew he couldn't just leave. They would wait for the morning, however long it took.

He sat listening to the night sounds, the deep-voiced frogs that reminded him of a men's choir, the wind whistling softly through the bush. Every once in a while he thought he could even smell smoke. He wondered if something outside was burning or if it was just from someone's chimney. Then he remembered it was the middle of summer.

People can't be that far off, he told himself, and then he heard something different, something out of place. An animal, maybe. Something walking through the bush toward them.

"Pa?" Patrick whispered, then held his tongue.

Michael said nothing, but when he stiffened, Patrick knew that his brother had heard, too. There was no use asking, so they quietly crawled behind a clump of mallee scrub bush and waited.

He knew for a fact he wasn't just hearing things when he saw the yellow glow of a lantern off in the direction of the balloon and the basket. The light stopped, but Patrick couldn't see who was holding it up.

Someone out looking for us? wondered Patrick. *Should we yell?*

But he couldn't; the shout was frozen in his throat as the footsteps grew louder and the lone tracker came closer with each step.

"Patrick?" whispered Michael, and Patrick squeezed his brother's arm to let him know he was there.

"Don't move," Patrick whispered into Michael's ear. Even a whisper seemed too loud as a long shadow spread over Mr. Graham's snoring body.

The sputtering lantern light showed the outline of a huge man, at least a head and shoulders taller than their father and twice as wide. He seemed to burst from his clothes. If Patrick had dared to stand up next to him, he guessed he might reach the man's belly button.

But he seemed to tiptoe through the bush in a way that showed he belonged. Or maybe he was just trying not to wake anyone at that time of night. He held his lantern between two fingers and bent down to stare at J. P. Graham. Only then did Patrick notice his face.

His brother's gasp told Patrick that Michael had seen the same thing. Patrick couldn't help catching his breath at the horribly burned face, either. The huge man had no eyebrows, no eyelashes, and not much of a nose. And the scars across his cheeks pulled what was left of his lip into a half smile that sent a shiver up Patrick's spine. But his large, dark eyes reminded Patrick of a frightened rabbit's. Innocent and scared, they didn't match the rest of his terrifying figure. Suddenly, the big, tanned man drew back in surprise; he'd seen them.

They must have stared at one another for several seconds. And Patrick couldn't tell who was more terrified: he and his brother, or the giant with the lantern.

Maybe this is the bunyip? he wondered. But now that he was so close to him, Patrick couldn't run or speak.

CHAPTER 6

FIRST RESCUE

"Hello?" Michael finally whispered.

"Don't talk to him," Patrick whispered under his breath, trying not to move his lips. He wondered if he and Michael could outrun the giant or what he might do to them if he caught them. Finally the enormous man started to back away.

"Who are you?" Michael blurted out.

"Shh," hissed Patrick. He reached up and clapped his hand on his brother's mouth to keep him quiet, but Michael pulled free.

"No. We need help," continued Michael. "Our friend, I mean this man here, he's hurt his shoulder. We crashed our balloon over there. And people are out looking for us."

Patrick pinched Michael on the arm to quiet him, but he only yelped and pulled away. The big man seemed to listen.

"Would you help us get back to our parents, please?" continued Michael.

Another long pause. Finally the man looked over his shoulder and held his lantern up high.

"There's no one else here," croaked Michael. "Just the three of us."

Still the big man checked all around them as if expecting to find more people hiding in the shadows. Finally satisfied, he inched back around—but his eyes still darted back and forth from the shadows to J. P. Graham to the boys and back to the shadows. He acted like a hunted animal. And he still had not said a word.

"Look at the size of those shoes," whispered Michael. Patrick took his eyes from the man's face long enough to notice two of the most enormous boots he had ever seen. A crooked toe stuck out of one, and both looked worn to the soles—not much better than going barefoot.

At least we know he didn't make those strange footprints between here and the balloon, Patrick told himself, taking a deep breath.

"I'm Michael McWaid." Michael stepped forward. "Are you going to help us?" Patrick couldn't make himself follow.

The man studied Mr. Graham once more but didn't answer Michael's questions. This time the balloonist snorted and his eyes fluttered.

"What?" began Mr. Graham, rubbing the sleep out of his eyes. He gasped when he noticed the huge shadow towering over him.

"Get away!" yelled the frightened balloonist, wiggling backward like an inchworm trying to get away from a hungry robin. "Get away, I say!"

I thought he couldn't move. Patrick could see pure terror on J. P. Graham's face as he reached for a stick and held it out in front of him.

"It's all right, Mr. Graham," said Michael. "I think he's going to help us get back."

"I doubt that very much," answered the balloonist, and so did Patrick for a moment when the big man advanced on Mr. Graham. The balloonist nearly fainted in pure fright but could go nowhere; he had wedged himself back against a bush.

"Mr. Graham?" Patrick wasn't sure what to do, so he sat frozen in place as the big man bent over the shaking balloonist. With his big hands he pulled Mr. Graham's arms away from his shoulder, pressing gently just below the neck, prodding with a couple of fingers.

"Oh! My shoulder!" yelped Mr. Graham.

What is he doing? Patrick crawled over curiously, watching as the big man placed his palm on J. P. Graham's forehead. His forehead wrinkled up in concern where his eyebrows would have been. Oddly, Patrick couldn't help thinking this giant of a man acted something like his mother did when Becky or Michael had a fever.

"If he's going to break my neck," mumbled Mr. Graham, "then he might as well get it over with."

Michael shook his head. "I don't think he's going to hurt you, Mr. Graham. Are you, sir?"

Still the giant said nothing as he stripped off his faded cotton shirt. The mighty muscles in his arms rippled as he tore it into long strips, then used the longest ones to fashion a sling for Mr. Graham's arm. A few more strips held the injured man's arm in place, flat against his chest.

"Well, I never . . ." huffed Mr. Graham, but he didn't protest when the big man helped him sit up.

"See?" asked Michael, picking up Mr. Graham's hat. "He's friendly. See?"

Michael tried a few more questions: "Where are you from? What's your name? What do we call you?" But the big man would not—or could not—answer.

"We know he can hear us," Patrick whispered to his brother as they watched the man gather tree branches. "Otherwise he wouldn't have stopped when you called at him."

Michael nodded. "Why do you suppose he doesn't talk?"

"Maybe he's one of those 'mutes.' People who can't talk."

"Everyone talks."

"I don't know, Michael. What's he doing now?"

The man had pulled out a long hunting knife. With swift, strong strokes he cut several nearby saplings and stripped the bark. Next he braided the bark into short lengths of rope and lashed the branches together to form a stretcher for Mr. Graham to sit in.

"Are you sure you can't walk, Mr. Graham?" asked Patrick. "You didn't hurt your legs, did you?"

"My dear boy," sputtered Mr. Graham, "this just goes to show you how very little you understand of the human anatomy. Everything is interconnected, and if my shoulder is injured, well . . ."

The big man worked on.

"Well . . ." For once, J. P. Graham seemed to run out of words. But he caught his breath and went on. "I told you, every bone in my body hurts. And I'll tell you, if I *were* able to walk, I certainly wouldn't sit here to have this odd fellow attack me."

"He didn't attack you," Michael assured him, but J. P. Graham didn't sound convinced.

"How do I know he didn't?" Mr. Graham waved his free hand at the stranger, who was down in the dust, finishing the stretcher. "After all, my memory of the incident is not entirely clear. And besides, *somebody* is going to have to pay for this embarrassment. What would people think if they heard that the great J. P. Graham had, well . . ."

"Crashed?" said Patrick. It was the wrong answer, at least according to J. P. Graham.

"No, no, lad. My injury is surely just the result of . . . rough handling."

Rough handling? Patrick wondered what the balloonist was trying to do. Looking for someone else to blame? Mr. Graham groaned as the big man lifted him like a doll and set him into place on the stretcher.

"My lucky hat, if you please," demanded Mr. Graham, reaching out his hand limply. "I never go *anywhere* without my lucky hat."

Michael dusted off the stovepipe hat and handed it back to Mr. Graham.

"Careful," Mr. Graham bellowed and planted the hat back on his head. "Now, keep to the smooth path, my boy, and take us *directly* back to Wentworth, do you hear? Keep away from the rocks and the bumps. Ow! What did I tell you? Easy, now. Easy, I say!"

Patrick and Michael looked at each other with frowns as the big man dragged Mr. Graham off through the bush. He seemed to know the way.

"I suppose we follow," said Patrick. "We'll explain what *really* happened when we get back."

The stranger still said nothing, only dragged the complaining balloonist faster and faster. He didn't even seem to need his lantern.

"It's not a race, I say!" shrieked Mr. Graham.

"I just don't understand why people aren't out looking for us," Patrick said.

The answer came a few minutes later, when Patrick heard a faint *pop* in the distance.

"There!" cried Michael, jumping in front of everyone. "Did you hear that? That was a gun."

"You're always hearing things, young man," replied Mr. Graham as they continued to bounce along. "Animal noises, guns . . . Next it'll be—"

"You heard it, too, didn't you, Patrick? They're out looking for us."

 MEETING THE GIANT

"I sure hope they *are* out looking for us," replied Patrick. He felt tired enough to fall asleep on his feet. But he ordered his legs to keep moving as the darkness gave way to a light gray dawn. He wasn't quite sure from which direction the sounds had come.

"As soon as we get back," said Michael, "I'm going to tell Pa about the weird noises we heard. What do you think it was? A bunyip?"

J. P. Graham nearly fell off his stretcher when the big man stopped and stared at Michael with a curious look on his horrible face.

"Keep going!" complained J. P. Graham, but the big man ignored him.

"Can *you* tell us about the bunyip?" Michael looked at the big man.

"We just heard these sounds last night," volunteered Patrick. "And from up in the air we saw this thing down in the bush."

From up in the air, thought Patrick. *That would make no sense to him.*

"It was big," tried Michael. He raised his voice and spoke more slowly as he stretched out his arms to give his impression of the creature they had seen from the balloon. "And it had a long neck, I think, and a really strange head. But then it disappeared."

The man just looked at Michael blankly.

"And now, if we're quite finished with this fascinating exchange," remarked Mr. Graham, the irritation sounding through his voice, "I'd very much appreciate continuing on—if you don't mind."

With that, the conversation was over. The big man's face clouded over again, and without a sound he turned back to pick up the stretcher.

"Easy, now, boy," said Mr. Graham. "Don't forget you have precious cargo here."

The man hurried on. Judging from the slowly brightening sky, Patrick guessed it might have been four or five in the morning. And before long he started hearing what Michael had heard earlier. Gunshots, then shouts.

"Patrick!" A faint voice floated through the quiet morning air. Patrick didn't recognize it, but that surely didn't matter. "Michael!"

With a new burst of energy, Patrick ran out ahead of the group. There was no mistake this time. He filled his lungs with cool air and cupped his hands to the side of his mouth.

"OVER HERE!" he shouted back and turned to the others with a smile.

"How about that," Patrick said. He couldn't keep the ear-to-ear smile off his face. "I *knew* my parents would be looking for us. Knew it all along."

"That's not what *I* heard you say." Michael offered his first smile in a long while.

"Go on, boy!" Mr. Graham ordered from his chariot. "Can't you see there's someone here to rescue me? At long last! That way, now! Watch the bumps."

Michael was the first to see the search party—an older man on horseback and two tired-looking young men.

"You found us!" cried Michael, running up to meet their rescuers. "I'm Michael!"

Patrick wasn't prepared for the greeting they got. Instead of smiles, the three searchers pulled back and stared at the big man. The jaws of the two younger men dropped nearly to the ground.

The older man pulled a rifle from a leather holster on his saddle. "We're looking for—"

"Us!" interrupted Michael, jumping up and down. "You were looking for us."

"Ah, excuse me." J. P. Graham cleared his throat and tried to turn around. "Turn this thing around, would you, boy?"

The big man stood still, looking at the ground, so Mr. Graham turned around himself and started waving at their rescuers.

"I say, do you know who I *am*? Yes, of course you do. Everyone knows J. P. Graham, the famous hot air balloon aviator. So glad you located me after a most uncomfortable evening in the wild. But no matter. The important thing is that I'm here now, and you'll provide me a way back to town, of course. I'm in need of medical attention."

The man on the horse lifted his eyebrow at them.

"Yes, naturally you will," continued Mr. Graham. "And my balloon. I'm offering a reward for the first ones to bring it back to the town. No rips or tears, though, do you hear? It's quite important that you treat my balloon with the utmost care. I can count on you, then?"

"A reward?" Finally the man on the horse must have heard something that made sense to him. Even so, he wasn't lowering his rifle, and Mr. Graham waved his hand as if to dismiss the rescuers.

"Oh yes, these people. This big beast here. Don't you worry. I have him under control now, although I wouldn't want to be around if he suddenly turned angry again."

Patrick gritted his teeth at the man's words but said nothing.

"Hmm." The grizzled old man surveyed them with a cautious eye.

"So now, my good man," the balloonist went on, "if you would kindly provide me with the use of your horse, I would be most grateful. Perhaps you'd like a ride in my balloon in return for your kindness? You'd like that, wouldn't you?"

The older man sucked on his teeth, scratched the stubble on his chin, and squinted at them before spitting into the dust and turning to one of his partners. "Ned, you and your brother follow their trail back to find their balloon. Wait there until I send a wagon to fetch it. I'll go back to town to tell them the boys are safe."

The two young men nodded nervously, backed away a couple of steps, then trotted down the path Patrick and Michael had just traveled. With the tracks from the stretcher in the dirt, it wouldn't be hard to find the balloon.

"Uh, your horse?" Mr. Graham looked up hopefully at his four-legged ride back to town. But the old man had other plans.

"I'll spread the word back in town that these two boys are all right," he told them. "Parents were pretty upset. Then, like I told my two sons, I'll send a wagon out after your balloon."

The way he said "balloon" told Patrick that the old man didn't think much of such foolishness. Still, there *was* the reward Mr. Graham had mentioned.

"When you get back," he told them as he wheeled his horse around, "we can talk about my reward."

"Uh . . . wait." Patrick was still curious. "You've seen our parents?"

The man nodded and kept sucking on his teeth. "They've been searching, all right. Just went back to Wentworth for more help, I believe." He gave them a salute and pointed his horse away.

"But—" Mr. Graham tried to object as their rescuer galloped off the way he came. "I insist you take me back immediately!"

The balloonist's pleas ended in a fit of coughing at the dust from the horse. Patrick didn't mind. They were almost to Wentworth.

"All right, now, that's far enough," insisted Mr. Graham as they neared the town. No one else had seen them yet.

"Don't you want us to take you straight to the doctor's office?" asked Patrick as they stopped.

"Well, now, that wouldn't look very good, would it? J. P. Graham, world-famous balloonist, being carried into town on a stretcher by a freak."

Michael scowled and planted his hands on his hips. "I don't like that word. It's rude."

"Oh, come, now." Mr. Graham ignored Michael's protest. "Let's just help me get to my feet, shall we?"

"You're going to walk?" Patrick asked. *After all that?*

Patrick had no choice but to help Mr. Graham up. The balloonist made a great show of tottering on his feet, groaning a bit, and using the boys for balance.

"There, now," he told them, checking a pocket watch. "Seven A.M. Perhaps I'll make it after all, despite our misfortune."

Patrick looked around for their big rescuer, who stood silently by the stretcher.

"You come with us to our paddle steamer." Michael looked back. "We can have breakfast, and you can meet Ma and Pa. Aren't you hungry? I am."

Patrick gulped and wondered what would happen if his parents saw the . . . He didn't want to use Mr. Graham's word: "freak."

"That's wonderfully thoughtful of you lads," chirped Mr. Graham. "Although I daresay your parents may not have enough foodstuffs to survive the challenge. How much do you think the beast will eat?"

"Stop calling him a beast!" insisted Michael. "You *are* rude!"

"Why, you impertinent little rascal." With his free hand Mr. Graham grabbed Michael by the ear.

CHAPTER 8

MESSAGE IN THE DUST

"Don't you hurt my brother!" yelled Patrick, rushing to Michael's side.

Mr. Graham only rolled his eyes and pulled back his hand.

"Oh, let's not overreact. We're all tired, I'm sure. However, I may have to speak to the local constable about you two after all, unless you behave yourselves."

"We didn't do anything wrong." Michael stuck out his bottom lip defensively. "It wasn't our fault the balloon took off."

"Not your fault that you jumped into the basket and caused the entire affair? Perhaps I shall have to press charges. I could force your parents to pay damages."

Patrick heard the threat. *He's blaming everyone else for what happened. Michael, the big man . . .*

"You can't get away with lying!" Patrick burst out before he thought of what he was saying. "Ma and Pa will believe us about what happened."

Mr. Graham just chuckled.

"Your mother and father, eh? Perhaps. Yet I daresay we'd all prefer to forget this entire incident rather than get the police involved, don't you think? Now, do we have an understanding?"

Patrick fumed. The big man came up beside Mr. Graham, standing between the boys and the balloonist. Patrick couldn't help feeling they had their own guard as they continued into town without another word.

They hadn't walked ten minutes, though, when Patrick heard a commotion in the street: Just around the corner, a man was giving a speech. Already several dozen people—mostly dock workers and young men—had gathered to listen.

"There, that's far enough." J. P. Graham pushed Patrick and the giant aside before he rocked on his toes for a moment and looked around at the gathering crowd.

"But what about your shoulder?" began Patrick. "Your arm's in a sling. I thought you were hurt."

This time J. P. Graham waved him off. "I seem to be recovering rather quickly."

"But—" Michael protested.

"Tut-tut," Mr. Graham cut him off and pointed his long finger at Michael's nose. "Not another word about this incident. I do have a reputation to protect."

Patrick and Michael looked at each other while Patrick tried to figure out what to do. It just didn't seem right. Nothing seemed right.

Mr. Graham went on. "And now I believe all these people deserve a ride in the wild blue heavens, don't you?"

The balloonist seemed to have forgotten his injuries and his threats as he strutted up to a young woman holding a parasol. Patrick could hardly believe what he saw, especially after the big man had dragged him all that way.

"Delightful morning, isn't it, ma'am?" crowed the balloonist. "Pardon me, but I'm J. P. Graham, the world-famous balloonist. Have you ever considered what an eagle might think as he's flying far above the clouds?"

Patrick rolled his eyes but was glad to see Mr. Graham disappear down the street, talking all the while to the unfortunate young woman. By that time, though, more people had gathered around them and were now pressing in from behind. Most stared with terrified looks at the big man, however, and walked in great circles around them. One little girl pointed and whispered to her mother, who pulled her back in horror. The giant stood out more than ever, and Patrick saw the look of a trapped animal in the man's eyes. The same look he'd seen when they first met him.

"You should come with us." Michael gripped the man's arm. "Our paddle steamer is just over there."

"Ladies and gentlemen!" boomed a man, the one who had attracted the crowd in front of them. He was balanced on a wooden crate and wore a wrinkled but gentlemanly black suit. It wasn't flashy like J. P. Graham's suit, but more like a banker's. And he wore his hair slicked back and wet, with a waxed moustache to match.

"Where do all these performers *come* from?" wondered a woman to their right. "And so early?" An old man next to her shrugged.

"Just the season for 'em, I suppose. Yesterday it was that balloon man, and now this bloke shows up on his wagon. Must've come in this morning."

"Now, ladies and gentlemen," boomed the man in the black suit, "my name is Dr. Phinneas Hume, recently arrived in your fair city from Adelaide. I'd like to give you a preview of what you may expect to encounter at my lecture this evening at half past seven on the practical uses of phrenology."

Patrick looked at his brother, thinking that they should leave while they could. The big man moved backward but stepped on someone's toes and stopped.

"And what, you will ask, is phrenology?" continued the man in the suit, his voice speeding up as he talked. "Well, madames and sirs, I have come to the conclusion after years of study that parents can save themselves much trouble and expense in training and educating their children by having a faithful analysis of their character. Will your Johnny become a criminal? Will your Susie go astray?"

Patrick looked across at the crowd of people to see if anybody else understood what the strange, swift-talking man was saying.

"What do you have," murmured someone from the crowd, "a crystal ball?"

Everyone chuckled, but the man on the box seemed to be just

warming up. He pointed straight at the heckler and leaned into his answer.

"Better than that, my friend. I've got the human head!"

Several people gasped.

"We should go, Patrick," Michael reminded his brother, but they were hemmed in on all sides and couldn't move. Patrick could only shrug.

"Yes, absolutely," continued Dr. Hume. "Your character, and the character of your children, can be determined through a detailed study of—" He paused for effect, tipped his hat and stared around the crowd, drawing them in even closer. "A study of their cranium, which only I, Dr. Phinneas Hume, can conduct."

He stepped back and put up his hands. "But I don't want to give away my scientific secrets. So please don't forget that admission to my lecture tonight is just a shilling, and after my lecture I'd be most happy to give anyone a thorough written analysis of their character for a mere ten shillings. Did you hear that, ladies and gentlemen? A *mere* ten shillings."

"Read someone's head right now!" yelled a man in the front. He stepped forward and bowed his bald head at the speaker. "Read mine!"

The doctor squinted at the man's head for a moment, frowned, and backed away as he shook his head. "Ah . . . no, my dear sir. I think for your sake we'd better not reveal your character to the crowd." He winked at the people standing nearest. "Wouldn't do to shock the good people of this fair town."

Of course everyone chuckled as Dr. Hume looked around. His eyes locked on the giant, and his face lit up.

"Ah, but I do see someone who would be most enlightening." He pointed straight at the giant. "You!"

For a moment Patrick didn't realize who had been singled out. But instantly the crowd parted, leaving Dr. Phinneas Hume to stride forward and face the big man.

"Behind the burns," boomed the doctor, "behind the ugly, grotesque scars you see here, there is a human soul and a story to tell. And now I'm going to tell it!"

If the giant's eyes had been wide before, they were now wild with fear. He shook his head violently and tried to back up, but there was no way to get through the wall of people.

"He doesn't talk," objected Michael. "He can't speak."

"No worries." The doctor lowered his voice and squinted at the giant carefully. He even reached out and held the giant's hand so he wouldn't back away. "I'll do the talking for both of us. You just tell me his name."

"I—we don't know," continued Michael. "He's—"

The doctor dismissed Michael with a wave. "Never mind, never mind. Just lean down here, friend, and let me see your head. No one's going to hurt you. I assure you, this is all in the name of science."

Or a good show. Patrick knew it wasn't right, but he couldn't bring himself to say anything. Instead, he wedged himself back into the crowd, away from the spectacle.

"Leave him alone!" Michael tried once more, grabbing the doctor's arm. But it was too late, and his little voice was swallowed up in the crowd's cheers.

"Enough, now!" barked Dr. Hume, raising his free hand. "I'll need complete silence."

The crowd obeyed as the doctor continued.

"Bow your head, my dear man," commanded the doctor calmly. The big man again tried to back up, but a little girl behind him gasped, and he couldn't move.

"Come, now." Dr. Hume tried once more. "We mustn't keep these people waiting. Bow."

With a helpless look to either side, the giant finally closed his eyes and bowed slightly, showing a shaggy mop of uneven black hair—thin in spots, bald in others, thicker elsewhere. Underneath, a patchwork of uneven scars showed through. No one made a sound except for a few cackles from older boys in the back and across the street.

"Oh!" Dr. Hume shook his head, as if startled, before he put his two hands on the big man's head and traced a line between three bald spots. "This is remarkable."

"Don't let him do this to you," Michael whispered hoarsely, but there was nothing he could do except look back at Patrick with teary eyes. "Why don't you *do* something?" he pleaded.

"Uh . . ." Patrick stammered and looked at his hands. "I would, but . . ."

"But *what*?" cried Michael. "You sound like you're trying to get out of doing the dishes."

Patrick bit his lip but didn't answer. *It's not my fault*, he told himself, but somehow he knew it wasn't quite so.

"No harm done, eh?" A yellow-toothed man sneered in Patrick's face, and his breath smelled like a stale saloon. "I'm sure the big fella can hold his own."

"Oh my," crooned the doctor, and the crowd followed his every move as he traced another line across the big man's shaggy head. "Just as I thought."

"No more!" shrieked Michael, and this time the yellow-toothed man shoved him hard back into the crowd. No one seemed to notice, least of all Dr. Hume.

"Yes, yes," continued the doctor, looking more closely. "But let me tell you something. My first examination leads me to tell you that this freak of nature has definite criminal tendencies. Unfortunately, it's very clear. A future criminal, I'm afraid."

"He is not!" protested Michael.

That announcement brought a few gasps from the crowd as the doctor dismissed them with a clap of his hands.

"That's just a sample. I can explain more tonight, if you like. So don't forget: half past seven tonight at the meeting hall. One shilling. Complete personal readings, ten shillings. Parents, I can read your children's *true* characters, which could save you considerable trouble and expense, could it not? We'll see you all tonight!"

Without another word he let the giant go as the crowd dissolved and people drifted back to their business. Michael rushed up to the big man, who was already hurrying down the street.

"I'm sorry they made fun of you," cried Michael. "I wanted to stop it, but . . ."

The big man wasn't listening.

"Wait!" cried Michael, trying to keep up. "Aren't you hungry? Can't you come to our paddle steamer? Please?"

But the man only put his head down and hurried off. Like a rat in a maze, though, he seemed confused about which way to go. A carriage bouncing down the street toward them brought him up short, and he wheeled around to face them.

"We don't even know where you live," Michael told him.

For a moment the big man's eyes narrowed as he studied the two brothers. His mouth opened, but no sound came out. Then, as he bent down as if to pick something up, another carriage went by on the street in a cloud of dust.

"Patrick!" a girl's voice rang out over the street sounds. "Michael! You're back!"

Patrick spotted Becky through the thinning crowd, a half block away. She lifted her skirt and ran down the street to meet them, dodging a couple of horses in the process.

"Becky!" shouted Michael, taking a few steps toward her.

Becky threw her arms around her youngest brother, pulling him off his feet. "We heard they'd found you," she told them, breathless. "Ma and Pa have been out looking for you all night. When I saw you disappear into that awful balloon, I thought we'd never see you again. *Either* of you."

"But, Becky," Michael pulled away from his sister, "you have to meet our friend . . ."

Michael turned to point out the giant, and his voice trailed off. "He was here a second ago."

Patrick looked up and down the street. How had the big man slipped away so quickly and so quietly? Becky gave them a curious look.

"He was here a minute ago, Becky, honest." Michael trotted up to a building and looked inside. The big man was nowhere to be seen.

Patrick sighed and was just about to kick at the dusty road, but something caught his eye. He bent down and traced the awkward letters in the dirt.

The big man had written something!

"Patrick?" Michael came up behind him to see what it was.

" '*K–o–o* . . . ' " began Patrick, taking care not to wipe away the letters. A man on horseback trotted their way, but Michael held up his hand like a constable directing traffic in downtown Dublin. The horseman grumbled but pulled around.

" '. . . *k–a–b–u–r–r–a,* ' " Patrick finished. He straightened up and clapped his hands together in a cloud of dust. "Kookaburra."

"What does a kookaburra have to do with anything?" wondered Michael.

Patrick scratched his head and stepped back to let another horse trample the mysterious message in the dust. Kookaburra? It didn't make any sense. *A kookaburra is a bird*, he thought, *but* . . .

"I don't know," Patrick finally answered, biting his lip and studying the horseshoe prints in the street. "I honestly don't know."

"Well, I know one thing, little brother," Becky told him as she looked down the street. "When Ma and Pa get here in a minute, you'll have some explaining to do."

CHAPTER 9

ACCUSED

"Better to explain everything back at the *Lady Elisabeth*." Ma hugged Patrick and Michael. Or rather, she nearly squeezed the life out of them. "After that absolutely horrible night of not knowing if you were alive or dead—" She dabbed at her eyes with a handkerchief. Her face looked red and blotchy, the way it always did after she had been crying. "We tried to follow, but it was too dark. We only just heard you had been found."

"But we weren't lost, Ma," explained Michael. Their mother shook her head and sighed.

"We're just glad you're alive, boys. And I want you to promise me you'll never, ever do anything like that again."

"It wasn't Michael's fault, Ma," Patrick defended his brother. "At least, not *completely*."

"I'm holding both of you responsible for getting into that balloon." Mr. McWaid's face was not red and blotchy, but he had dark circles under his eyes, and his clothes were dusty and wrinkled. He gripped the backs of the boys' necks as they marched down Wentworth's main street, back to the wharf. "And that irresponsible Mr. ... whatever-his-name-is who was piloting that contraption. In fact, where did you say he was? I'm going to have a word with him."

"No, Pa, please." Patrick shook his head and tried to slow down, but he could only drag his feet in the dusty street. "Pa, you don't want to talk to him. He's a little . . . well . . ." Patrick wasn't sure how to explain J. P. Graham to his father.

"He's really different," Michael explained as he pointed to a storefront office. "And I think he might be over there."

Arthur Jameson, M.D. was written in an arch of fancy gold lettering on the window of a small office wedged between a blacksmith's shop and a dry goods store. As they came closer, they could hear loud voices inside.

"He was this tall, I tell you!" J. P. Graham limped out of the office, lifting his one free arm high over his head. Though his other arm was wrapped in a new white bandage and sling, he moved it around freely. "But the crafty beast managed to slip away."

A man in a dark blue police uniform followed Mr. Graham out into the street. The elbows of his jacket were frayed through, and his beard could have used a trim, too. He stood with his arms crossed and traced a pattern in the street with his scuffed boots. Pa finally loosened his grip on the boys.

"So what you're telling me, Mr. Graham," drawled the officer, "is that you landed safely out in the bush in your balloon, and this big fella just came up out of nowhere and attacked you and the two boys."

Mr. Graham took a deep breath when he noticed the McWaids.

"That's exactly correct, Officer, but I'm not certain if I'll press charges this time." He smiled broadly. "Perhaps we'll just let bygones be bygones."

"That's him, Pa," Michael whispered to his father. "That's J. P. Graham. He's trying to blame everybody but himself."

"Mr. Graham," began their father, hurrying his pace. "I'll have a word with you. I—"

"Ah, but you must be Mr. and Mrs. McWaid," the balloonist greeted with a broad smile. "I've heard so much about you."

Patrick's mother didn't pull back quickly enough to keep Mr. Graham from grabbing her hand and raising it to his lips.

"Delighted to meet you both," crooned Mr. Graham. "You have two very courageous young men here. They'll make excellent aerialists someday."

The constable cleared his throat in the background. "Begging your pardon, ma'am, and Mr. McWaid, sir, but I just thought you'd want to know that Mr. Graham here is considering dropping all charges against the big fellow that attacked them out in the bush."

"Attacked?" Mrs. McWaid gasped, still not understanding. "The boys said nothing about being attacked."

"What's this?" demanded Mr. McWaid.

J. P. Graham silenced him with his free hand. "Please, sir, there's no need to worry. They were under my protection during the entire flight. At no time was there any hint of danger. And as I always say, all it takes is good looks—"

"And a little cleverness," echoed Patrick, "to overcome any problem."

"Ah yes." Mr. Graham looked surprised. "That's it. Now, as I was telling the dear constable, I suspect the poor beggar was hungry. Perhaps he thought we were a threat, like a mother bear protecting her territory."

Michael scratched his head. "He was no threat. He was nice."

Patrick decided it would not be a good time to tell anyone about the bunyip sounds.

"Are you speaking of the big fellow with the awful burned face?" asked a man who was walking by. He seemed to shudder as he spoke, and his expression told Patrick that, yes, he had probably seen the giant.

"You saw him?" asked Mr. Graham, interested in what the man had to say. The stranger nodded energetically, and his beard flapped up and down.

"Sure did. And that head-reader fellow, he said he was a criminal of some sort. Someone should tell the constable about him, even though he looked harmless enough."

"Ah," said Mr. Graham, "appearances can be deceiving."

"Listen here," answered the constable. "If the man didn't do anything wrong, and if Mr. Graham isn't willing to press charges, there's nothing I can do."

The stranger's eyes widened. "That's just it. He's hardly what you could call a man. You'd know what I'm saying if you saw him, right, Mr. Graham?"

"Well, now, I don't know just what I would say, sir. To be charitable . . ."

Charitable? thought Patrick, the heat of anger rising in his cheeks. *J. P. Graham is talking about being nice to people? That's a new one!* Then he thought about how he himself hadn't stood up for the big man, and he held his tongue.

"He helped you when you were hurt," Michael blurted as he stood just behind his father. "And he dragged you all the way into town. Don't you remember?"

Patrick's father put his hand on his youngest son's shoulder.

Mr. Graham laughed nervously. "Didn't I tell you, Constable?" The balloonist pulled off his tall hat long enough to mop his sweaty crop of hair. "I told you the children wouldn't understand what a threat this fellow was at the time, did I not?"

The constable nodded his head. "Yes, you did, but are you sure—"

"Of course I'm certain." He turned again and winked at Mr. McWaid. "I wouldn't want to involve the boys in any more trouble, you see. That's why for now I'll just let this matter drop. Better for everyone this way, wouldn't you agree, sir?"

Mr. McWaid scratched his chin and looked at his three children, then back at the balloonist. "I appreciate your concern, Mr. Graham, but—"

"It's the least I could do." The balloonist held out his good hand with a toothy smile. "Truly a pleasure. After taking these . . . ah, stowaways for a ride, I was, of course, determined to bring them back safely to you, and I want to assure you that we were never in any danger up there. In fact, when I get my balloon reassembled and aloft again, I'd like you and your wife to come up for a ride with me, at no charge. I'm sure you'd enjoy the experience, especially when you consider the savings."

He bowed low, then cried out with pain and nearly fell on his head.

"Oh dear! My shoulder. Doctor?"

A small, balding man rushed out the door of his office and helped J. P. Graham straighten back up. The balloonist smiled.

"There, now. The good doctor assures me I'll be all right, after all. Sturdy stock, as my grandmother would have said. You'll join me tomorrow, then?"

"Don't do it, Pa!" Michael whispered into his father's ear. Patrick would have said the same thing.

"No, thank you, Mr. Graham. We've got a paddle steamer to load, and then we must be on our way. But thank you for taking care of my boys."

"Ah, but it was the least I could do, Mr. and Mrs. McWaid. Why, it reminds me of the time we were in Mozambique, and the chief of the natives there . . ."

J. P. Graham didn't seem to mind who listened to his tall tales, so he continued while the McWaids excused themselves and hurried back to the wharf. The last Patrick could hear of the balloonist was how the view of Wentworth from his world-famous balloon looked just like the mysterious countryside around Mozambique, and how the doctor and the constable could each experience the exhilaration of a ride into the clouds for a special price of just ten shillings. It reminded Patrick for a moment of the phrenologist, the phony head reader.

"And for you, my friends, I'd like to offer you a special opportunity at a greatly reduced rate from that normally enjoyed by the regular public."

Maybe Mr. Graham and the head reader are working together, he wondered, but the thought of what J. P. Graham had said about the big man snapped him back to reality.

"That's not how it happened at all, Pa," Patrick said when they were far enough away so J. P. Graham couldn't hear. He took turns with Michael, explaining to their parents how they had landed, how they had found Mr. Graham in the dark, and how the big man had come and cared for Mr. Graham's hurt shoulder.

"This big fellow doesn't sound like a bad sort," Mr. McWaid told them. "Why didn't you bring him here to meet your mother and me?"

"That's just it," explained Patrick. They swung on board the *Lady Elisabeth*, which was waiting patiently at the wharf. "He ran off when he saw we were all right. And he *was* a bit scary, his face and all. I didn't know if it would have been a good idea."

Michael scowled at him, while Ma put her arms around their shoulders once more and squeezed them tightly.

"Well, giant or no giant," she said, "the important thing now is that we have you back safe where you belong. Isn't that right, John?"

Patrick's father didn't answer as he stared back at the wharf.

"John?" His mother picked up on Mr. McWaid's worried expression. "What's wrong?"

John McWaid shook his head and didn't look back. "The wool's still not here. And neither is Jefferson."

They didn't have to worry long about what could have been wrong. Less than an hour after they returned to the *Lady Elisabeth*, Patrick saw Jefferson hop off a wagon, wave his thanks to the driver, and hurry over to the boat.

"Well, look who's back!" The stocky, square-faced American greeted Patrick and his brother with a big, toothy grin and a stinging slap on the back that made Patrick grin and wince at the same time. "Everyone thought you had flown off across the country. Maybe you were going to try for China?"

"We almost did," replied Patrick. "We flew over . . . Wait—you left for the station before we took off. How did you know what happened?"

Jefferson shrugged. "The fella who gave me a ride told me."

"You should have seen it, Jeff," piped up Michael. "We could see *all* the way to the ocean, and maybe farther."

"Not *that* far, Michael," Patrick corrected him.

"But it was *far*. And everything looked really tiny, like—"

Patrick nudged his brother with his elbow and shook his head—a quiet signal that they had better let Pa do the talking just now.

"Glad you're back," interrupted Mr. McWaid. "What about our wool?" He kept his eyes trained on the wharf. It was still empty. "What did you find out?"

Jefferson held up his hands when everyone crowded around him for the news. "All right, I'll tell y'all what's going on. I think we may be in big trouble."

CHAPTER 10

JOURNEY TO KOOKABURRA STATION

Jefferson seemed to enjoy telling his story almost as much as J. P. Graham would have.

"Some kind of mutiny at the station," he explained, shaking his head. "I didn't get the whole story, but the shearers aren't getting fed proper. The whole thing is slowing everybody down, and word is they're going to pack up and go someplace else."

"Someplace else?" Mr. McWaid clenched his fists. "What about our wool?"

Jefferson could only shrug his shoulders. "Most of it's still on the sheep. They're way behind schedule, says Mr. Glover."

"What about Mrs. Glover?" asked Ma.

"There *is* no Mrs. Glover," Jefferson replied with a shake of his head. "He's a recent widower, and it's just the men. So I told them . . ." His voice trailed off, and he scratched his chin. "It seemed like the only thing to do, so I . . . uh . . . volunteered us."

Silence. Mr. McWaid looked more closely at Jeff, almost nose-to-nose.

"Us?"

"Yes, sir." Jefferson cleared his throat and looked at the deck. "I figured our only chance of getting that wool would be to . . . do something. Cook, maybe?"

"And you told them?"

"Yes, sir. Actually, I told them you'd be there by midday."

"Today?"

"Yes, sir. I'm sorry if I . . ."

Mr. McWaid glanced at his wife. If they were going to get their wool and keep their paddle steamer, perhaps this *was* the only way.

"Let's do it, Pa!" shouted Michael, jumping up and down. "Let's go to the sheep station! Christopher will love it." By that time he had found his pet koala, and the poor little animal was having a hard time hanging on to Michael's shoulders, especially with his filed-down claws.

"Not you," Mr. McWaid told them. "You young ones will stay here on the boat with Jeff."

"Actually, sir"—Jefferson sounded ready to apologize—"they would be a help, as well. Fetching, running errands. I said they'd come."

"All of us?" Mrs. McWaid planted her hands on her hips to register her "no" vote to the idea. "But we just found the boys. And they've not slept all night."

A nod from Mr. McWaid told Patrick to pack his bedroll.

"If we don't get that wool soon, dear, you know what will happen." Mr. McWaid's quiet arguments were usually enough to convince their mother. She nodded.

"I'll get some food together," volunteered Becky.

"And I'll get Christopher ready to go," added Michael.

"No, Michael. Your koala has to stay here," Mrs. McWaid said. "Becky, I'll help you with the food. You boys need to change out of those muddy clothes!"

"Yes, ma'am!" Michael sounded eager to return to the bush country. But as Patrick rolled his blankets tightly together, he noticed a faint, slightly familiar smell.

"Do you smell something burning?" he asked Michael.

His brother stopped wrestling with Christopher for a moment and sniffed at the breeze coming in through the open side window of the paddle steamer.

"Could be. But there's always something burning in the town."

Patrick shook his head. "No. This is different. It's the same kind of burning I smelled on the way back from the balloon crash."

"I still can't smell anything. Here."

Michael threw his bedroll at Patrick, sending Patrick stumbling backward. He caught himself on a side wall and launched the roll back as hard as he could.

"Boys!" His father called down from the outer deck. "Are you almost ready?"

"Coming!" Michael shouted back.

Patrick stuffed some clothes into a sack and tied it all together with a short piece of rope. But he sniffed the air once more and wondered. It *was* getting smokier, and something about the air made Patrick feel uneasy.

It would take a little more than an hour to reach the station in their rented wagon, so Patrick dozed in the back. Ahead and behind stretched rolling flatlands, covered in waist-high brush and the occasional lonely tree. Patrick had seen it before. To the side was more of the same as they followed a well-worn set of wagon tracks. Still, thought Patrick as he opened and closed his eyes every few minutes, it was oddly beautiful—just like the rest of this land.

"Kookaburra Station is just up ahead," announced Jefferson from the front seat. Patrick sat up and started choking—not so much from the cloud of dust in his face as from the older boy's words. *Kookaburra Station.* He could still see the big man's message in the street.

This has to be what he meant, thought Patrick. He caught his breath and rubbed the stinging dust out of his eyes to get a better view. Maybe it wasn't such a coincidence after all. There weren't many places to go from Wentworth. For certain, not many called Kookaburra.

It was easy to pick out the main house at Kookaburra Station, with its rusted metal roof and comfortable-looking wide veranda. A pot with a dried yellow flower sat sadly by the closed front door, another victim of the hot spring.

"This is it?" wondered Becky.

The house could stand a new coat of whitewash, thought Patrick, and the windows were impossible to see through. Beyond the house, most of the other buildings were scattered on top of a little hill as if they'd been blown there, tumbleweed-style. One of the ramshackle buildings was made of stone. Another—no, two others—were slapped up with weather-beaten bush lumber full of knotholes and none too straight. Yet another shed had hardly any walls at all, just crude boards tacked on one end and swaying in the gentle breeze that bathed the station. However, the biggest of these sheds was a long and low, well-built sheep barn, and it was filled with activity.

Outside the sheep barn, men on horseback were whistling and shouting, cutting their horses back and forth in front of panicked sheep. Darting around their feet, brown-and-tan sheepdogs did their work of herding the woolly creatures into place. All the sheep from miles around funneled into a pen. Patrick could not take his eyes off the sight.

"I've never seen so many sheep in one place," he whistled softly. His father brought their rented wagon to a dusty halt and looked around. Most of the sheep they saw were fully covered with a thick carpet of shaggy, off-white fleece. In one of the pens, however, a collection of pink-skinned, sheared sheep stood still and shivering.

"Kookaburra Station," announced Jefferson the same way train conductors call out destinations. "This is the end of the road."

It *looked* like the end of the road, as well. Glancing around, Patrick noticed puffs of dust in two or three directions, more men and more dogs, all headed toward Kookaburra Station. Jefferson helped first Becky, then Mrs. McWaid, down out of the wagon.

"Amazing." Patrick stood up in the wagon and turned around to take it all in. He was the first to notice a sturdy, bowlegged man limping toward them, a concerned smile on his face.

"G'day." The bowlegged man was covered with sweat and grime, but he wiped his hand on the side of his dungarees as he approached Mr. McWaid. "I'm Vince Glover. Been expecting you."

"John McWaid." Patrick's father took the hand he was offered and pointed at his family. "You've met Jefferson. This is my wife, Sarah, and our children, Rebecca, Patrick, and Michael."

"Grand," replied the man. "We're a little late delivering your wool, so you've come to collect it yourselves, have you?"

The question must have caught Mr. McWaid off guard, or else he wasn't ready for the man's blank expression or his blunt challenge.

"Oh no, I mean, yes, we are, but I didn't mean to offend," Pa stammered. "Jefferson said you could use a little help, is all. Perhaps speed things up a bit?"

"John, we shouldn't have come," said their mother quietly, and Patrick noticed her back was as straight as a flagpole. She didn't move from her seat.

Maybe we should turn right around and go back to Wentworth, thought Patrick.

CHAPTER 11

FINDING IBBY

Vince Glover put his head back and laughed.

What's funny? wondered Patrick, slumping down in the back of the wagon.

"Don't mind me." Then he turned back to the McWaids with a smile. "We're glad you're here, especially if you don't mind helping out. Fact is, these shearers are ready to leave tonight if they aren't fed properly. They were expecting my wife's good cooking, but . . ."

His eyes filled with tears, and he swallowed hard.

"I'm sorry," he sniffled. "It's been six months since she passed on, but . . ."

"We're very sorry," said Mrs. McWaid, and he nodded his thanks.

"Well, the cook I hired disappeared," continued Mr. Glover, "and I tried cooking, but it was worse than nothing at all."

"Well." Jefferson dusted off his clothes. "That's why we're all here."

"Settled, then." Vince Glover pointed to an outbuilding with a crooked black pipe poking out of the roof. "The cookhouse is over there, and we could use a few extra roustabouts over on the shearing floor. These young people ever done anything like that before?"

"I can be a roustabout," Michael answered before Patrick found his tongue. "What's a roustabout?"

Again the man laughed. "You're a little young, my boy. But if you've come to work, as your father says, you'll find out right quickly what a roustabout is. The men will teach you, probably faster than you want to be taught."

Patrick looked around quickly before he jumped down. No sign of the big man, but there were plenty of buildings he could be in. After everyone had made their proper introductions, Patrick found himself following the jolly Vince Glover across the courtyard in front of the main house, dodging barking dogs and shouting men on their way to the shearing shed.

"Hello there, Red." Their host waved at one of the men as they walked. "And you there, Jim, don't let those sheep loose."

He turned aside, as if telling a joke. "Last year we spent half our days chasing after those crazy animals."

Mr. Glover knew all the men, and each one gave a cheer when they heard a new cook had finally arrived.

"A proper meal tonight?" said one, a tall, sunburned man with a thick moustache. "Maybe we'll stay after all."

"Count on it, mate," answered Mr. Glover. "And the McWaids will be staying with us a day or two."

We will? wondered Patrick. But then he supposed if they were going to be helping with the wool, it *could* take a while.

"These are musterers," Mr. Glover explained as they threaded their way through the confusion. "Their job is to get the sheep from the outside into pens and, from there, to the real action. Come on."

A pair of dark eyes peeked out at them from inside the barn as they walked to the large main door.

"Ducks on the pond!" a voice shouted from inside the barn. The call was repeated, then again.

"Ducks?" Patrick looked at their host, who smiled and pulled back the door with a grunt.

"Shearers are a rough lot," he explained, "but they're sure enough polite to the core." He nodded at Becky, who held Michael's hand. "I expect you wouldn't want to hear their carryings-on before a nice sheila like your sister walks in. It's just their way of warning the gang to watch their language, you know? Ladies present."

Sheila. Patrick thought for a minute when he heard the Australian slang. *A lady. I've never thought of Becky that way before*.

"I still don't know what ducks they're talking about," wondered Michael, pulling on his sister's arm. Jefferson grinned.

"Don't you see?" Becky bent down to explain to her brother with a smile. "Looks like I'm the duck. Quack!"

Patrick stood in the doorway, his eyes adjusting to the half-light of the shed. Bright golden shafts of sunshine filtered in through cracks between the boards to reveal a symphony of shearing, with a dozen conductors holding wicked-looking shears. Stripped to the waist and sweating freely, the dozen or more men stood in a long line, each one wrestling a wriggling, struggling sheep. Their hands flew as they expertly snipped carpets of fleece. And three or four boys—Mr. Glover called them the "roustabouts"—scurried between the rows of trimmers, scooping up the precious fleece and running it over to a wool-rolling table. To Patrick it all looked like a wild, loud game.

"Sort of a big wool factory," shouted Mr. Glover, raising his voice to make himself heard over the din.

And oh, the noise! Michael plugged his ears, as if that would help keep out the racket of dogs barking, clippers clacking, sheep bleating, and men shouting. Becky chose instead to hold her nose at the powerful animal smells.

"Over here, boy!" One of the shearers was building a knee-high pile of fleece and pulling up another ewe to his clippers.

"Wool away!" yelled another. "Shake that broom, lad!"

The others whistled and waved as the musterers drove in sheep after frightened sheep from the outside. No one let up, no one slowed down, and the shearers seemed as if they would shear their own fingers as quickly as they would relieve the sheep of their fleece. For their part, the sheep put up as much resistance as they could, especially when they were nicked by the shearers or bullied by the dogs, who yipped and nipped at them constantly.

"Good dogs, those." Mr. Glover jerked a thumb at the pack. "Good shearers, too. Maybe the best in Australia, if you ask me. But since you didn't, I'll tell you anyway."

One of the men, a stooped little fellow who looked as if he had been hunched over in the same position for years, glanced up with a toothless grin. He never missed even an inch of fleece, and Patrick suspected the man could have sheared his animals to the bare skin even if he were blind.

"There's no dozen men on the continent that can shear a mob quicker'n these fellas," continued Mr. Glover. "I'm lucky to have 'em before they move on to the next station. But you have to feed the blokes right or else."

"Or else what?" asked the shearer.

"Else Ibby'll come after us," Mr. Glover teased. "Isn't that right?"

"Who's Ibby?" wondered Becky, still holding her nose.

Mr. Glover crossed his arms and scratched his dimpled chin before he answered.

"Now, don't be alarmed, miss. They say he's harmless, and I've never seen anything to convince me otherwise. All I know is he's the fastest shearer in New South Wales, probably in all of Australia, if I had to lay money on it. But he's a bit of a scare the first time you see him."

With that warning he pointed with his eyes to a hunched figure on the far end of the line, put his fingers in his mouth, and whistled loud enough to be heard over the din.

"Say, Ibby!" he shouted. "Got some folks here who want to meet you."

Patrick had not noticed him before; the man was as tall hunched over double as the others were standing upright. Becky gasped when Ibby paused over his sheep and looked their way. Even Jefferson's eyes grew wide, but he stood his ground.

"It's him!" cried Michael. He scooted past the line of shearers and around several piles of wool to meet the big man. There was no mistaking him.

"Michael, be careful," Becky warned, but there was no need.

"You know Ibby?" Mr. Glover looked confused.

"He's the one who helped us get back to Wentworth this morning," Patrick explained, "after our balloon crashed. He dragged the balloon pilot for miles. But then when we got to town, he disappeared."

"A balloon, eh?" Mr. Glover crossed his arms. "Doesn't surprise me a bit. Ibby's always out wandering, looking for lost sheep or birds to rescue. You were probably the next best thing."

Patrick could hardly believe they had found the big man, or . . . Ibby. But then again, it made sense. Where else but Kookaburra Station? Mr. Glover kept up his explaining.

"The fellas all say he's a few bales short of a load, if you know what I mean. I'm not so sure." Mr. Glover chuckled. "But if you've met him out in the bush, you've discovered Ibby is not the most talkative man in the world."

"Ibby?" Patrick craned his neck back to see into the big man's eyes. He wasn't sweating like all the others, and he was the only one who wore a shirt, neatly buttoned to the top, though the sleeves were much too short. "Is that his name?"

"Real name's Ibrahim," explained Mr. Glover. "All we know of him is that his parents were from Afghanistan or some such place, and that he's all alone here on the other side of the world. Really a shame about his face, you know, as if being such a giant wasn't enough."

Jefferson whistled. "Looks as if a steam boiler blew up in his face."

Ibrahim towered awkwardly next to Michael, who shook his huge hand in a greeting and looked up at him like a long-lost friend. Mr. Glover didn't stop talking.

"I can never figure if he just doesn't want to speak English or can't, or if he doesn't have a voice at all. Which is it, eh, Ibby?"

The giant Ibby, or Ibrahim, acted as if he hadn't heard the question, but he let Michael shake his hand and nodded seriously at his little friend.

"Well, would you look at that." Mr. Glover shook his head. "I've never seen the big fella shake anybody's hand."

Maybe because no one's ever offered, guessed Patrick, but he didn't say anything. They made their way past the lineup of shearers to the end. Silently Ibrahim bent over, picked up his shears, and continued his work while they stared.

"How does he do that so fast?" wondered Becky as Ibrahim shaved first one, then two and three animals in nearly less time than it took to describe. Soon there was a tall pile of fleece next to him.

"The other shearers are good," agreed Mr. Glover with a nod, "but Ibrahim, he's a magician."

"It's like he's shaving his own face." Jefferson couldn't take his eyes off the artist at work. And neither, it seemed, could the sheep. Where the other men sweated and cursed at their animals, Ibrahim seemed to paralyze them with his grip and hypnotize them with his stare. One after another, the sheep lay at Ibrahim's feet, quivering, while he fleeced them.

"I tell you, I can't watch for very long." Mr. Glover turned away. "Otherwise when I get back outside, I'll have to check my own head of hair to make sure Ibby hasn't trimmed it off in the bargain."

They all stared at the show. Without thinking, Patrick put his hand up to his red hair just to make sure it was all there, too.

"You three can help in here," Mr. Glover told them as he turned to go. "Jeff, you come with me. Got some work outside you can do with rounding up the animals."

Jefferson nodded and followed, but Mr. Glover halted by the door, remembering something.

"Only mind your fingers around the shearers. You want to come out of the barn with ten of them, just like when you walked in, eh?"

He put his head back and laughed again, an odd sound among all the shouts and animal sounds of the shearing barn. Ibrahim went right on shearing sheep.

"I've never seen anything like it," whispered Becky. She was as fascinated as Patrick and Michael. Five sheep turned to ten, and still they kept coming until Ma appeared at the barn door with a tray full of teacups. As if on cue, the shearers all looked up and stopped what they were doing. All but Ibrahim.

"Tea, all!" announced Mrs. McWaid.

"Well, now." One of the shearers grinned and took a cup. "This is more what I had in mind. Glover, he about burned the tea water when he tried it."

"I assumed you boys like your tea on the strong side," Mrs. McWaid told them. "Hope you don't mind."

A dozen sweaty shearers and the roustabouts eagerly took their tea in long swallows, gripping the chipped china cups awkwardly in their big hands.

"I'll bring in the cups," volunteered Becky, and Ma smiled her appreciation.

"That's good, dear. We have a lot of work to do."

Without another word she bustled out of the barn, leaving the big door to slam behind her. Michael studied Ibrahim as they sipped their tea, and the big man didn't seem to mind the curious stares.

"How do you get them to sit still like that?" asked Michael. "The sheep, I mean."

Ibrahim shrugged, shook his head, and stared at the dusty floor. But it was the first time Patrick had seen him answer any of their questions directly.

So he does understand, thought Patrick. *He has to*.

"What about those shears?" Michael wasn't going to give up so easily. "How did you learn to use them like that? Back in . . . where are you from?"

"Michael," Becky scolded him as she collected teacups, "don't pester him so."

"I'm not pestering him," Michael defended himself. "I'm just asking him questions because I want to know. That's not pestering, that's just asking."

"But he can't answer you," Patrick whispered in his brother's ear. Ibrahim raised his head slowly, and when he looked at them, Patrick was afraid he would go limp like one of the sheep.

Did he hear me? wondered Patrick as Ibrahim picked up his shears and towered over them. Patrick swallowed hard, but he still couldn't read the man's odd, twisted face. Patrick took a step backward without thinking, and Ibrahim grabbed at him.

CHAPTER 12

RUNAWAY BRUMBY

"Oh!" Patrick didn't have time to think as he lost his balance and began to tumble over one of the sheep. Despite his giant size, Ibrahim moved faster than Patrick fell. Before Patrick hit the floor he grabbed Patrick by the front of his shirt and pulled him back to his feet. Patrick wasn't sure whether to thank the man or run.

"I guess I'm a little clumsy," Patrick finally managed to stammer as he brushed off his shirt and backed away.

Ibrahim grunted quietly as he let Patrick go, then he checked with his thumb to see how sharp his shears were.

"I'd best be helping Ma." Becky's tea tray trembled, and she nearly stumbled as she backed away. Michael didn't seem to notice what was going on.

"Mr. Ibby," he asked in his regular curious-excited voice, "you want me to tell you about the bunyip we saw again? I'll show you what the tracks we saw looked like."

Michael started tracing a shape in the dust, but Ibrahim shook his head and wiped out the shape with his hand. Carefully he drew another shape, like a wide seashell the size of a large dinner plate, notched on the bottom with two marks. He scalloped the edges with the tip of his shears, using them like a pencil, before he stood back and nodded at his drawing.

"That's it!" Michael smiled and pointed at the drawings. "Isn't that what we saw out there, Patrick?"

Patrick studied the prints. "Sure enough they are, Michael. That's what we saw. But what kind of creature would make such a footprint?"

Patrick's voice trailed off when Mr. Glover burst back into the barn, clapping his hands.

"All right, mates, let's get back to the shearing. You know how far behind we are. We need to finish up soon so the McWaids can take the wool downriver. You heard Mrs. McWaid is cooking for us tonight, eh?"

The dogs started barking again, and the noise in the barn began to rise once more. Ibrahim jumped back to work, as well, pinning the next sheep in his lineup. Patrick looked at his brother.

"So much for that conversation. What do we do now?"

As if to answer Patrick's question, a man crashed through the side of the barn from the outside and landed on his back in a pile of wool. His eyes nearly popped out of his head, and he pumped his feet as if he were still running. Outside, a horse whinnied and bucked, followed by more than the usual shouting and barking.

"Hold down the mare!" yelled someone as the man rolled over on his side and groaned in pain. The unshaven, wiry-looking fellow couldn't have been older than twenty. For only the second time since Patrick and his family had arrived at Kookaburra Station, the shearers dropped what they were doing to watch the show.

"Are you all right?" Patrick rushed to the man's side. The young station hand was gasping and gripping his side, but he nodded.

"No worries, mate," gasped the man, struggling to find his wind. "It takes more than a little kick in the ribs to slow me down."

With that, the man grinned and brushed away a shearer's offer of a hand before pulling himself to his feet.

"But say, Roger," said one of the shearers, pulling another sheep into place and starting his work again, "you could have at least used the barn door."

"I'll remember that," agreed the young man.

The others laughed at the joke and returned to their work, as if that sort of thing happened all the time. The man who had come crashing into the barn brushed the slivers out of his hair and limped back outside, where four or five others had surrounded his black horse. They formed a human fence around its wild, riderless dance.

"I said, hold it down!" barked Mr. Glover, advancing slowly on the wild-eyed animal as it snorted and bucked. "Roger, haven't you broken this brumby yet? We don't have time for this sort of nonsense during shearing. You just need to—"

"Working on it," mumbled the rider, still rubbing his side. "I thought she was broke."

Obviously she wasn't. The horse breathed hard, nostrils flaring, and tried once to break out of the circle. The men were just as determined to hold her in, though, and began to tighten the circle. But when one of them reached for the animal's harness, it reared back on its hind legs, pawing wildly at them.

"Easy, there!" yelled Mr. Glover. "No one gets hurt."

Patrick and the others watched from the new "door" in the side of the barn as the men closed in, then retreated, then once more tried to hold the horse down. But not even the rider could calm the wild horse.

This time Patrick wasn't surprised when he felt Ibrahim brush by him. Michael tapped his brother on the shoulder as the big man silently stepped up to the scene.

"Watch what happens now."

Sure, and how could I take my eyes off this? Patrick asked himself.

"Back off," warned one of the men in the circle as Ibrahim approached. "What do you know about wild horses?"

"Say, there, what's he doing with my horse?" asked the man named Roger, the one who had crashed through the barn.

Ibrahim ignored the comments and kept his eyes locked on the wild animal in what must have been a direct challenge. The horse looked away and pawed wildly at the ground.

"Let him through," Patrick found himself whispering, but it didn't matter. Ibrahim pushed the men aside as if he were walking through bushes. They watched in silence as Ibrahim began a sort of dance with the mare.

As Ibrahim advanced on the wild-eyed horse, Patrick found himself silently praying for him. Even though man and horse stood almost eye-to-eye, everything about the wild fury of the untamed animal frightened Patrick.

"He's going to get kicked, just like the other fellow," said Michael. Patrick held up his hand to quiet his brother. Ibrahim stepped toward the animal, then turned on his heel and strolled away. Still breathing hard, the horse flicked her tail nervously but followed. She obviously understood his silent language.

"How does he *do* that?" wondered Michael.

Again Ibrahim repeated the steps to his dance: Turn around with arms crossed. Stare at the nervous mare until she looks away in confusion. A couple of steps closer, then turn and walk away. Each time, the horse followed closer, as if she were being led on a rope. Or maybe it was the little flat cake Ibrahim held in his hand. The horse sniffed and pawed at the air, eager for a taste.

In just a few minutes the horse was so close he could have touched her. Finally Ibrahim held the animal's reins and stared straight into its eyes, for he was just as tall as the animal. For a moment Patrick thought the horse would fall over, dead or asleep, chewing happily on the little treat.

"Think the Arab's got some sort of spell?" wondered one of the men who had been trying to catch the horse before. Roger was red in the face. Patrick shook his head, not sure what to think, until Mr. Glover broke the awed silence.

"Good show, Ibrahim," he said as he grabbed the reins from Ibrahim and passed them over to the young rider. "Now, Roger, you keep a tight rein on this brumby from now on, do you understand?"

Roger glared at everyone, then stuffed a wide-brimmed hat on his head and tugged on the reins with a mean shake before leading his horse away. Ibrahim silently turned back to his work, no expression on his face to hint at what he might be feeling.

"All right, now," Mr. Glover continued. "Let's get to it! We have a lot more wool to shear before this day is over."

Which was true, as the sheep kept coming and coming through-
out the rest of the afternoon. Jefferson saw to that. Patrick and
Michael watched Ibrahim for a while longer and even helped some
of the roustabouts collect sheared wool. But by suppertime they
were ready to join Becky, Jefferson, and their parents inside the
station house.

"All cleaned up?" their mother quizzed them as they walked in.
Michael stomped his feet of dust, just as he saw the others doing.
Patrick held up his hands to show he had washed, too, and his
mother nodded as they sat down at the long, dark mahogany table.

"Absolutely, Mrs. McWaid!" Jefferson pretended to spit in his
palms, then held up his clean hands with a smile. "We washed outside."

Supper at Kookaburra Station wasn't quite as lively as the
shearing, but close. Patrick counted more than twenty plates. Including the McWaids, that would mean a place for Mr. Glover, another man called Uncle Ned, who looked a lot like Mr. Glover but
didn't say much, and a shy little boy named Nathan. Jeff sat between Michael and Patrick, and he looked hungrily around the
table.

A dozen shearers joined them as Mrs. McWaid began serving
bowls of steaming food. Only Ibrahim wasn't there. And one chair
sat empty until Roger came strutting in after they were all seated.
He dusted off his wide-brimmed hat, tousled little Nathan's hair,
and picked up a fork.

"Have any more trouble with the brumby mare, Roger?" asked
Mr. Glover, passing a steaming plate of meat to his left. Roger shook
his head and stabbed at the meat as if he hadn't eaten for days.

"No worries, Pa," he mumbled.

Pa? Finally Patrick was beginning to understand who was re-
lated at Kookaburra Station. Even before the strong-smelling meat
had made its way around the table, Roger started to shovel the food
into his mouth as fast as he could manage.

"The fellas are pretty happy about getting an honest meal finally," he told them. "Not bad. Not bad at all."

Several of the men murmured their agreement. Jefferson added his "mmm" to the chorus.

"Son." Mr. Glover cleared his throat as he poured himself a glass of water from a pitcher. "You're forgetting your Glover manners."

"Eh, what?" Roger looked up from his plate as he chewed.

"As you can probably tell," mumbled Mr. Glover, "things haven't been the same around here since my wife died. We very much appreciate your help, Mrs. McWaid."

Ma smiled and nodded.

"No need to apologize," replied Mr. McWaid.

"Are you going to ask a blessing?" Michael asked his father, not too loudly, but loud enough for everyone to hear. Roger dropped his fork with a clatter.

"Ow!" he cried, looking at his father. "No need to kick me."

The station owner ignored his son's protests, put down his glass of water, and nodded at Mr. McWaid. A couple of the men took off their hats.

"By all means."

Mr. McWaid didn't seem to mind. "Father in heaven, we thank thee for thy provision for us today," he prayed in his comfortable, deep voice. Patrick never doubted that God could hear his father. "For the fruit of this good land, and for the faithful family here who labors so hard. We ask thy blessing upon the work of their hands, and . . . that they may know thee and thy peace. In Jesus' name, amen."

Patrick looked up at his father just in time to catch the wink of his eye and a half smile out of the corner of his mouth. Roger voiced a loud "amen" with his fork in midair, then attacked his food again.

"Very good mutton," he said as he shoveled in another mouthful.

That's what it is, thought Patrick, giving his sister a quick look. *We're eating those poor sheep*.

The grown-ups talked about the shearing and how they would be loading up the last of the wool for its journey down the river.

Jefferson put in a few stories about how the wool here was just like the cotton in Arkansas, and he made them all laugh a time or two.

Patrick thought of all the sheep Ibrahim had so gently sheared and wondered which one had been unlucky enough to find the butcher's knife, as well. He had to admit, the meat *was* good, even if it had a strong, unusual taste. But when he looked at Michael's plate, his brother hadn't eaten a bite. Their mother noticed at the same time.

"Michael," she said, giving silent orders with her eyes, "how are you liking the meat?"

Michael's eyes watered, and he bit his lip to keep it from quivering.

"Michael?" Their father looked up from his conversation with Mr. Glover. "Are you well?"

Finally the boy could hold it in no longer, and he burst out in tears.

CHAPTER 13

THE CAMEL TRAP

"Michael, whatever in the world?" Mr. McWaid pushed out his chair and stood up. Mrs. McWaid pulled him back down.

"But I thought they just sheared the wool," blubbered Michael, letting the tears fall into his plate. "I . . . I didn't know."

"You didn't know *what*?" Mr. McWaid's expression clouded over in concern, or perhaps embarrassment. Mr. Glover looked bewildered. Roger smothered a chuckle behind his napkin.

"I d-didn't know we were going to *eat* the sheep," Michael finally admitted, and at that Mr. McWaid relaxed back in his chair.

"Oh, is *that* all." He looked at their hosts with an apologetic shrug. "It's my turn to apologize for my boy. He's quite fond of animals, you see."

"It's not a sheep." Roger leaned across the table with a big piece of meat on his fork, pointing it straight at Michael. Gravy dripped to the tablecloth.

"Roger!" gasped the young man's father.

"Yeh, see? It's camel meat. Not sheep at all."

Patrick choked.

"Roger," Mr. Glover scolded his son. "That's quite enough. You mustn't torment the lad with your stories."

Roger finally leaned back with a laugh, but not before he had popped the meat into his mouth. "Mmm. It's even better than lamb. Isn't it, boys? You should try it."

Michael sat frozen in his seat, staring at his plate. A couple of the men chuckled. After a few moments he started picking around the edges, working at his potatoes.

"Don't worry, Michael." Becky tried to make him feel better. "You don't have to eat it if you don't want to."

Patrick didn't know what to make of the situation, and he studied Roger out of the corner of his eye. Finally he couldn't help wondering.

"What do you mean by camels?" Patrick blurted out. "Have you ever seen one?"

"Sure, I've seen one. Haven't you?"

Patrick had to shake his head.

"Big ugly monsters. Long neck. Slobbery mouth. Stupid as a rock, which is only a shade brighter than all those sheep." He waved his hand toward the barn. Outside, the night was beginning to close in.

"You see them around here?" Michael finally spoke up.

"Oh no." Mr. Glover laughed, trying to break the tension. "Camels are from Africa, of course. We don't have them here in Australia."

"Yeh, but—" Roger held up his fork, still chewing. "I've heard a couple of beasts from the last overland exploring expedition were turned loose, and they're out in the bush somewhere."

"You mean there are real live camels out in the bush?" Patrick thought about it for a moment, and he wondered what kind of sounds they might make.

"You should ask your Arab friend." Roger laughed once more, but his laugh wasn't light or pleasant like his father's. "He'll tell you all about it, I'm sure."

"Your father told us Ibrahim was from Afghanistan," Becky said softly, "not Arabia."

"Yeh, whatever." With that, the young man grabbed his hat and pushed back his chair. "Good camel, Mrs. McWaid."

He grinned and left, leaving his father stuttering.

"You'll have to excuse Roger," he told them. His face was flushed. "He's really a good boy, just a little . . ."

"High spirited." The silent Uncle Ned finally spoke up with a scowl. "And about as easy to tame as those brumbies he likes to ride."

Roger hadn't shut the door tightly behind him, but no one seemed to mind the simmering hot evening breeze that slipped in through the door from the courtyard. Of course, the ever-present noises of the sheep slipped in, too. Patrick strained his ears for something else. This time he wasn't as afraid to hear the cry of the bunyip.

"You heard that Roger fellow," Michael whispered to Patrick in the darkness of the hay barn, where they were sleeping with some of the shearers. "It's not a bunyip out there. It's a camel. That's what we saw from the balloon."

"Hmm." Patrick wondered how long they had been sleeping. Two hours maybe?

"I'm going to go catch him," Michael continued. One of the shearers snored in the corner.

"Catch him?" Patrick rolled over. "Are you serious? Go back to sleep."

"Just think." Michael sounded like a circus announcer, and Patrick wasn't sure where he found his energy. "If we capture this camel, we could take people on exploring expeditions into the desert, just like the explorers, like John Stew."

"You mean John Stuart. And you've been listening to too many stories."

Patrick couldn't help chuckling at his brother. He had to admit that, for a nine-year-old, Michael had a head full of ideas. Not many of them were very practical, but still . . .

"Shh!" Michael suddenly clamped his hand over Patrick's mouth, and Patrick heard it, too. Footsteps coming their direction, toward the barn.

"Hide," whispered Michael.

"That's silly," Patrick answered back. "It's probably just—"

Patrick lost his voice when he saw a tall, dark figure filling the doorway of the barn. He stood for a moment, outlined against the starry night sky outside, then ducked his head to step inside.

"Ibrahim!" Michael called quietly to their friend. "We didn't hear you get up."

Ibrahim—if it really was Ibrahim—stopped for a moment in the doorway, looking almost bigger than life. He made a soft grunting sound and stepped in.

"We were going to ask you before," Michael chatted as if they were old friends, "but we never got a chance. Do you know anything about catching camels?"

Ibrahim paused where he stood.

"You know, big furry animals with a hump on the back? They make sounds like this, don't they?"

Michael did his best imitation of the strange sound they had heard before in the night. Ibrahim finally smiled and nodded his head. Patrick could barely see the gleam of the man's teeth in the dim light from outside.

"Michael says he wants to catch the camel." Patrick decided he might as well talk to the big man, too, as long as he didn't get too close. "Isn't that the silliest thing you ever heard? What would we do with a camel, even if we caught it?"

"I told you, Patrick." Michael wasn't going to give up. "We'd start a guide service. Explore the whole continent. Be the first ones to go from north to south. We'd be famous."

"It's already been done, Michael." Patrick rolled his eyes, knowing his brother wouldn't see him in the dark. "Don't you remember? That's where this camel came from, if there really is a camel."

"Of course there's a camel. You heard it."

"Maybe so, Michael. But you can't capture one just like that."

"And why not?"

While they were arguing, Ibrahim turned back to the door. Before he stepped outside into the soft night, though, he grabbed a coil of rope hanging on the wall, then motioned for them to follow.

"What does he want?" wondered Patrick.

"I don't know." Michael was the first to follow. "But I'm going to see!"

Patrick had almost forgotten how hard it was to follow Ibrahim across the outback, how the big man seemed to cover at least three of their steps in one of his, and how he almost ran when he walked.

"Don't run so fast," puffed Patrick.

"Hurry, Patrick." Michael called from up ahead. It seemed almost wrong to shout in the still, beautiful night, but Michael and Ibrahim were getting too far away.

"Coming!" Patrick began to run. The stars were so bright, he could almost hear them humming, and when a shooting star blazed from east to west, he was certain it roared.

Or maybe it's the camel again. Patrick stopped and stood completely still, the only sound his heavy breathing. By the light of the stars, something looked familiar about the short trees, the thick grassland, the smell of water.

"Over here, Patrick!" Michael called from up ahead.

"I didn't realize we were so close to the water hole," Patrick huffed as he finally caught up to the other two and looked around. "This *is* the same place, isn't it?"

"The balloon landed over there, I think." Michael pointed at the edge of the water hole, and they tiptoed over to a soft spot in the mud.

"I remember." Patrick nodded and noticed something else. "But look here. Fresh wagon tracks. Men from Wentworth must have hurried out here and pulled that balloon out already."

Ibrahim was kneeling by the water several yards away.

"What is he looking at?" wondered Patrick as they wandered up behind the big man. As usual, he didn't say anything, but he took Patrick's hand and with it traced in the soft earth.

"What is this?" asked Michael, kneeling closer. It was hard to see in the dark, but they both could tell Ibrahim was trying to show them something.

"A track?" guessed Patrick, and he lowered his face to the

ground. Again and again, Ibrahim dragged Patrick's hand over two large shapes, each one like a bell.

"It's the camel track," whispered Michael.

Patrick finally understood. "A camel track, not a bunyip track."

But now that they had found where the animal had been, Patrick wasn't sure of what to do next. Did Ibrahim want them to wait there in the darkness, wait for the camel to come along for a drink. . . ? Then what would they do?

"Here's where we set our trap, right?" Michael straightened up and followed Ibrahim to a nearby stand of saplings. For the next half hour, they helped him rig a man-sized snare, using the coil of rope and a sapling for a spring. Working almost as quickly as he sheared sheep, Ibrahim carefully looped the end of the rope, covered it with leaves, and carved a trigger out of two pieces of wood.

"The camel steps here," explained Michael, getting down on all fours, "and the loop gets him around the leg, like so."

Michael pretended his leg was caught in the loop and jumped up with his leg held high in the air. Ibrahim smiled for the second time. Actually, he almost laughed out loud.

"I don't think this is such a good plan." Patrick rubbed his chin. "Maybe it would work for a little animal. But don't you think a camel would just break loose?"

He picked up a walking stick and poked it at the trap just to see. Without warning the loop closed around Patrick's stick, yanking it from his hand in one swift movement. Patrick hopped backward with a yelp.

"Whoa!" he cried. "Maybe it *will* capture a camel."

Michael laughed, but Patrick had only made them more work. Without a sound Ibrahim pulled the stout sapling back down into position, and they set the trigger again. This time Patrick stayed a more respectful distance away and watched as the big man pulled something from his pocket.

"What's that?" asked Michael, and Ibrahim held out a thick, flat pancake—the same thing he had offered the wild brumby horse. When Michael still didn't understand, Ibrahim nodded and held it out even closer.

"Horse breakfast," whispered Patrick. "Maybe you didn't notice how much the horses like that stuff. Try some."

"No . . ."

Ibrahim must have understood Patrick's joke; with a twinkle in his eye, he bit off a corner of the hard cake and held it their way to sample. Finally Michael took a little bite.

"Hmm, pretty good." Michael chewed and chewed. "Sweet. Tastes like treacle."

Patrick liked treacle—molasses—as well as anybody. But he also didn't want his teeth to break off from chewing the hard-as-rock horse treat. He watched as the big man wedged it under the trap's wooden trigger.

"I *told* you it would work," said Michael. "The camel can probably sniff our molasses bread for miles."

"All right. Maybe it does work. But I still don't know what we would do with a camel, even if we do manage to loop this rope around its leg and don't end up with a mad dingo dog."

All the way back to the station house they argued the possibilities, hardly aware that Ibrahim was with them—except when the big man stopped and sniffed the air.

"Do you smell that, too?" Michael asked Patrick, and Patrick took a couple of deep breaths through his nose.

"I smell it. Smoke. Same as before."

Their guide could obviously smell the smoke, too, and he stopped every few minutes to sniff the air. Even in the starlight he looked worried.

"The wind is changing," announced Patrick, licking his finger and pointing it up into the air. This time there was no mistaking the sharp, eye-watering bite of smoke.

CHAPTER 14

SOMETHING IN THE AIR

Back at Kookaburra Station early the next morning, even the sheep seemed to sense something was wrong. They wandered aimlessly and bleated as if they were lost. Patrick stared at the animals as he and Michael and Becky watched the shearing before breakfast. Jefferson was already out bringing in the animals.

"They're fidgeting about something," said Patrick, and the others nodded. It couldn't have been later than six or six-thirty, but already the hot dust was hard to breathe.

"Maybe it's the dogs," guessed Becky, pointing at one of the noisy animals the men directed with shouts and whistles.

"Maybe," agreed Patrick. "But even the dogs look nervous."

As if to prove the point, one of the dogs nipped a sheep in the back of the leg, sending the terrified animal sprinting into the shearing shed. Someone roared from inside.

"How many times do I have to tell you?" shouted a man. "You're always in my way!"

Patrick tiptoed to the shed, followed by his brother and sister.

"And you know what else, big fella?" hollered the man. "I've about had all I can take of you. Doesn't matter to me if you *are* the fastest shearer in Australia."

Inside the dim shed they could see Roger, the station owner's son. Looking up at Ibrahim, he was shoving the big man back with each word. They couldn't see Ibrahim's expression, but they didn't need to. Michael was the first to move.

"You can't do that to Ibby!" Michael called out and pushed his way into the shed.

Roger looked up at the interruption with fire in his eyes. By that time, though, Michael had stumbled over a bundle of burlap sacks and was beside his big friend.

"Out of my way, boy," growled Roger, pushing Michael back into the sacks. "This is between me and him."

"He didn't do a thing," Becky spoke up. "And he's surely not hurt you."

Roger just sneered at her. The others in the shed stood statue-still, staring.

"Isn't he your friend?" Michael asked the shearers as he got to his feet. The sacks were soft and had cushioned his fall. "Aren't you going to help him?"

The men looked at the ground, and still no one said a word.

"He's the owner's son," someone mumbled. Still, Michael didn't move out of the way. Finally Roger backed up a step, wiped the sweat with his dirty sleeve, and showed his teeth in a sort of grin.

"I think the man without a face is big enough to take care of himself," he said.

Obviously Ibrahim could have, had he wanted to. Instead, he quietly returned to his sheep.

Jefferson poked his head inside. "There a problem in here?"

Patrick never had a chance to answer, and the others never had a chance to get back to work. Before Patrick could open his mouth, a man on a sweat-lathered horse galloped into the courtyard. At first he looked as if he were dressed in black, but in a moment Patrick realized the man was covered in soot. He reminded Patrick of a chimney sweep.

"Wildfire!" announced the man, his voice hoarse. "Headed straight this way!"

The news hit Kookaburra Station like a lightning bolt, and everyone ran outside. Becky looked up at the sky toward the west and gasped at the billowing cloud of black smoke. She gasped as the chaos of sheep, dogs, men, and horses turned downright crazy. While Patrick and Michael helped the news bearer's weary horse, Becky picked up her skirt and ran for the house.

"You people have to get out of here," continued the man in black. Even his face was covered in soot. By the way he slumped in the saddle, Patrick guessed the man had been riding for hours.

"How far—"

"Listen, boy," interrupted the rider. "I've no time to tell stories. The wildfire's headed this way almost as fast as a bloke can ride. I wouldn't linger over breakfast if I were you."

Wildfire? Patrick wasn't surprised, not after what they had seen from the balloon and had smelled for the last few days. But that didn't keep his heart from racing at the thought. The rider swallowed hard.

"Winds are whipping it fierce. You tell your people to clear out with whatever they can carry. But clear out!"

One of the shearers dropped his tools and turned back to the barn just as Mr. Glover came racing out of the house. Becky was leading her parents out at the same time.

"What's all this?" wondered Mr. Glover, scratching his head. The dark horseman looked toward the smoke wall, sighed, and wheeled his horse around nervously.

"Already told the lads here." He pointed to the west at the now obvious wall of dark clouds. It looked like a mass of thunderclouds to Patrick, only much more evil looking.

"Then tell *me*," insisted Mr. Glover. The rider frowned.

"You've got only a few hours before the flames reach this station. Maybe not that long. I'd run for the river. The water may stop it, or it may not."

"Ah, no worries, mate." Mr. Glover batted the news away with his hand. "The grass around here is too sparse to burn much. Just a little grass fire is all it is. I've seen 'em before."

"Not like this one, you haven't." The horseman pointed at the flames. "The wind is whipping it into a lot more than just a little grass fire. Look for yourself. But don't look too long."

"I've seen this kind of fire before, sir." Jefferson gazed at the clouds with a worried look. "We'd better do as he says."

"But—" Mr. Glover started to ask another question, but the horseman obviously wasn't in the mood for a chat. All the shearers by that time were lined up at the shed door, watching. Even Roger stood silent, his mouth wide open, as the rider disappeared at a gallop down the dirt road to Wentworth. A cloud of dust followed him. Everyone turned to Mr. Glover, who squinted at the smoke. A roustabout's hat tumbled across the courtyard.

"All right," Mr. Glover finally sighed. "I can't keep you shearers from leaving since you don't work directly for me. And of course, Mr. McWaid, I don't expect you and your people to stay. Load your wagon with as much wool as you dare."

"But what about you, Mr. Glover?" asked Mrs. McWaid. "You're not going to stay here, are you?"

Mr. Glover nodded his head. "We're going to fight it, if what that fellow says is true. But don't worry. She'll be right."

Who is she? Patrick wondered until he remembered the Australian expression *She'll* be right, meaning *It* will be all right. After what the horseman had told them, Patrick wasn't so sure.

No one moved for a very long minute—until Jefferson pushed his way out of the barn with a couple of buckets in hand. He paused at the animal watering trough, dipped the buckets full, and trotted back to the wool barn to douse the wooden siding.

"Well, let's don't just stand here." Mr. Glover broke the strange silence. "Let's give the bloke a hand."

Jefferson's move woke everyone from their daze. With a shout the other shearers ran to find their own buckets or any tool they could get their hands on.

"You men come with me!" bawled Mr. Glover. "Jefferson, you too! We'll clear a strip of land to stop the flames. All you others, get everything wet so a spark won't set us afire."

As their host ran off, Patrick glanced quickly at his parents; his mother clutched her husband's arm, and his father's forehead wrinkled in worry.

"Are we going to leave?" asked Patrick.

At first his father didn't take his eyes off the approaching column of smoke. Then he bowed his head and led a prayer for Kookaburra Station. For the Glovers. For the shearers. And for Ibrahim.

"And please don't let the sheep get hurt," added Michael after their father had finished.

Patrick couldn't help smiling. When he looked up, he saw Jefferson staring at them from a distance. The older boy winked and turned back to his shoveling.

"All right." Mr. McWaid raised his head and flew into action. "Now, remember, no matter what happens, everyone *must* stay together. That means Patrick and Michael, especially."

Patrick nodded his head as his father continued.

"I'll get our wagon ready just in case. But first let's see if we can help. Becky, you stay with your mother. And, boys, you're with me. We'll have some bread and cheese as we go."

"Right, Pa." Patrick nodded at his father's instructions.

"Get all the sheep together!" shouted a roustabout. Patrick fell over as one of the panicked animals ran into him from behind.

"You think it's bad now, fella," Patrick whispered to the animal. "I'm afraid it's only going to get worse."

But just how bad? The black-brown cloud seemed to carry its own lightning as it roared before the wind, heading straight toward Kookaburra Station.

The next two hours passed in a blur of panic and shouting as everyone did what they could to prepare for the attack of the fire. Patrick and Michael mostly followed their father with buckets, wetting down anything that might burn. About a dozen men helped Mr. Glover in the impossible job of clearing away bushes and trees in a wide strip around the station houses and barns.

"I don't see how . . ." Becky paused to watch the men for a moment. She obviously didn't want to say it, either. But there was no way they could clear away everything that would burn. At least not before the flames arrived—flames that raced toward them like a fiery express train. Jeff waved back at them as he swung his shovel like a hoe.

"There they are!" Patrick was the first to actually see the flames, sometime around nine o'clock. He pointed to a line of low trees around a dried-up creek bed less than a mile away, where smoke had begun to rise.

"I don't see it," muttered Michael, but then they all stared as the tinder-dry trees exploded into flames. Now they could hear the roar, even from a distance. Patrick's mouth went dry, and the wind grew even stronger, smokier. In a few minutes it closed in like a roaring, choking fog.

"John . . ." Their mother looked at Mr. McWaid with a worried glance. Jefferson and the men on the front line were frantically clearing brush, but they had a long way to go. On the other edge of the station, the McWaids' wagon sat waiting and hitched. Two horses pulled nervously on their bridles.

"We're ready to go, dear, as soon as . . ." His voice trailed off. Patrick noticed something orange and about the size of a firefly drifting down out of the dark, cloudy sky.

"At least the roof is tin," said Mr. McWaid, hefting another bucket of water and dousing the ember. A second ember followed, then another. One even landed on Becky's head, and Patrick swatted her with his hand.

"Ouch!" he yelped, feeling the spark burn his palm. Becky ducked and shook her head, but by then the sparks were showering down like a plague of locusts.

"Over there!" yelled Michael, pointing at the barn. A group of sheep huddled behind a small fence next to the building. None had yet been sheared, and one of the largest was running in circles, flames shooting from its wooly back. The terrified animal filled the air with its pitiful scream.

Without thinking, Patrick grabbed his sister and sprinted to the sheep pen. Michael was hollering and pointing and jumping up and down.

"Water!" screamed Michael. "Douse it with water!"

Which of course was easier to say than do, as the flaming sheep never stopped running in circles. Becky heaved her bucket of water at the animal, but it was moving too quickly. The water splashed another sheep in the face, who sputtered and backed up while the living torch kept running in utter panic.

"Oh no!" Becky dropped her bucket. "Now what?"

"We can't just stand here and watch," wailed Michael.

No, we can't. For just a moment Patrick thought about the mutton they'd eaten the night before. But now his stomach turned at the sight of the terrified animal and the sound of its horrible cries. He vaulted over the fence and launched himself in a flying leap at the sheep.

"Hold still!" yelled Patrick, and he managed to grab one of the sheep's hind legs—then the other. Ignoring the flames, he dug his head into the animal's side and drove it into the dirt, kicking and protesting.

In no time Patrick was on top of the poor sheep and all four of the animal's legs were straight in the air. Patrick lunged with all his weight to keep the animal on its back, smothering the flames in the dirt.

"Hold him there!" cried Michael as he slipped between the fence railings and joined his older brother. Together they pinned the helpless animal to the ground until Becky pulled them back.

"It's out," she told them, and they watched for a moment as the sheep pedaled its four legs in the air. When the sheep scampered away, all they could see was a black spot on her back where the ember had caught fire.

"Becky!" shouted Mrs. McWaid from the other side of the courtyard. "We need your help over here!"

Patrick snapped back to reality at the sound of his mother's call, and they rushed back to where she was swatting embers in the bushes with a broom. Their battle against the advancing fire was far from over; embers were now falling on them like rain. Flames burst from the dry brush all around them. The roaring sound was getting louder.

"Get yourselves wet," Pa told them as he doused Mrs. McWaid

with a bucket of water. She in turn soaked Becky, and Patrick dumped water on Michael.

"Normally I'd get in trouble for this," muttered Patrick.

Another ember lit like an angry fly on Michael's wet shirt but flickered out before it could do any harm.

Wet clothes, thought Patrick, and it reminded him of something he had stumbled upon in the shearing shed.

"Follow me," he told Michael, grabbing his brother's hand. "I've got an idea."

CHAPTER 15

FIGHTING THE FIRESTORM

Getting through the shed was no easy matter, however, as it was packed with animals from wall to wall. Over the sheep's bleating and the cows' bellering, Patrick heard another sound he couldn't identify.

An animal? he asked himself. *No, it sounds more like somebody whimpering.*

But there was no time to wonder about noises. Patrick squeezed his way through the animals, frantically searching for the pile of burlap sacks Roger had pushed Michael into just hours before.

"See those sacks?" he said to his brother. "We need them."

A minute later they were back out in the courtyard, sacks in hand. Quickly Patrick soaked them with water and began attacking both embers and small fires.

"I hope this works," shouted Becky, taking one of their wet sacks. She swatted the side of the house to put out a hot spot.

It had better work. But Patrick was almost afraid to look at the yellow-orange glow that now lit up the smoke that poured in on them. He tried to cover his mouth with a wet handkerchief and take short, shallow breaths to keep from coughing so much. Wet sacks or no wet sacks, the flames would surely wash over them in just a few minutes.

"John. . . ?" Ma's glance toward the waiting wagon was all that was needed. Mr. McWaid wiped his brow and squinted through the smoke at the men still working between them and the advancing flames.

"I know, Sarah. I know."

Patrick knew, too, but he kept swinging his wet sack at anything that glowed. The bushes and dried plants were the worst; they went up like a torch if he didn't beat out the spark soon after it touched down. He couldn't imagine what would happen when the dried grasses that surrounded them turned into a carpet of fire.

When it comes, he told himself, *not if*. He could feel the heat pushing through the smoke. He resisted the temptation to turn and stare at the firestorm, which came sweeping directly toward them as if aimed by a giant, blowing the flames right at Kookaburra Station. Sometimes it almost leaped like a wild animal; then it would settle down to a crawl. But always it came closer and closer.

"Pa, look at that!" Michael pointed to flames licking up the side of a storage shed on the edge of the property. One of the flying embers had found a safe place to land and grow.

"I'll get it." Patrick dunked his scorched burlap sack one more time, ran through the blinding smoke, and attacked the flames.

"Watch it!" yelled a man, coming up behind him and dousing the flames with a bucket of water. Patrick turned to see Roger Glover. His face was smudged and sweaty.

"Thanks," Roger told him. "But you should be leaving with your family."

Patrick shrugged, then continued beating sparks. "All the shearers are helping out. We thought we'd try, too."

"Where's your big friend?"

Patrick nodded toward the line of men in the smoke. He couldn't see Ibrahim but figured he was probably at the head of the crew.

"I'm sorry," began Roger. "Maybe I shouldn't have . . ."

Patrick knew he was trying to apologize for treating Ibrahim so harshly earlier. "You should talk to him yourself. But there's no time for that now."

There wasn't even time to eat, and still they were losing their battle with the advancing flames. By the side of the house, Becky batted away a smoldering pile of dry branches that had blown in and lodged just underneath one of the windows. The wind freshened up again, and now flames were in plain sight, screaming over a low hill just beyond the meager firebreak.

"The firebreak isn't wide enough." Patrick shook his head and watched the flames advancing. The wind funneled hot clouds into their faces.

"Buckets!" shouted Jefferson from the trench. "We need more buckets! They're in the shed."

"I'll get them," replied Patrick before anyone else could volunteer. He was happy to escape the smoke and flames for a moment, and he raced into the cool sanctuary of the dark shearing shed.

Where are they? he wondered, searching the dark corners for any sign of buckets. *There!* He spied a dozen or so, stacked in the corner. But a rustling sound in the shadows stopped him.

"Hello?" Patrick hesitated. "Anyone there?"

The stack of buckets fell over with a clatter to show Ibrahim crouched in the corner. A glimmer of smoky daylight from outside caught his horribly burned face, and for a moment Patrick thought he was looking at a trapped animal.

"Oh, it's you." Patrick inched to the corner. "I just came in for some more—"

"We need those buckets, son!" hollered a man from outside.

"Coming!" Patrick kept his eyes on Ibrahim as he gathered up the buckets. He wondered what might have burned the man's face so long ago and if it might have been a fire like the one now threatening them.

"It's all right." Patrick turned to go back outside. "I don't blame you."

Ibrahim stayed where he was, nearly curled up in the corner. His fear-filled eyes told Patrick everything he needed to know.

A moment later Patrick was back outside with the buckets. They were not going to make any difference, though.

"John, we have to leave," choked Mrs. McWaid, falling to her knees and pulling her burlap sack to her face. "Before it's too late!"

As their mother spoke, Becky's sack burst into flames, and she dropped it with a scream. A stranger stepped out of the smoke from the far side of the station.

Who's that? Patrick wondered, looking back and forth from the shearers and roustabouts working with Mr. Glover. *What are they doing back there?*

But then another man emerged, and another, each one hurrying toward them with a shovel over his shoulder.

More arrived on horseback, shouting and whistling, pointing at the advancing flames. Many were wearing town clothes: white shirts, shiny leather shoes, and hats. And they met the flames like an army.

"Say, Roger!" shouted one of the men, waving his shovel at them. "Looks like you need a hand!"

Roger grinned from ear to ear and trotted up to greet the newcomers. "What are you all doing here?"

"You didn't think we were going to miss this, did you?" the man called over his shoulder as he headed for the fireline. "Some of the blokes brought some meat to cook over the fire. Thought we'd have a regular picnic supper."

Patrick had a hard time smiling at the man's jokes, so he went back to battling the blaze. At the same time, two of the men from town dragged a flat scraping plow behind a team of two steady black draft horses. Ignoring the almost unbearable heat of the approaching flames, they scraped clean a wide track of the dry bushland. Ten more attacked the flames with their tools, pouring dirt and hacking bushes out of the way.

But even with the extra help, it wasn't long before Patrick could tell it wouldn't be enough.

"The flames just keep coming," he whispered to no one in particular, and his words turned into a prayer. "Lord, we can't stop this. But these people can't lose their station."

He looked at Jefferson beating desperately at the flames as a yellow tongue of fire jumped across the line and a dozen men scurried to get away. Mr. McWaid glanced up, dropped his wet sack, and took Becky by the arm.

"That's it," he yelled to Mrs. McWaid. "Let's go!"

But this time it was Mrs. McWaid who stopped. With a puzzled expression she put up her hand and seemed to search the smoky air.

"What is it, Sarah?" asked their father, but Patrick already knew. He could see the smoke clearing somewhat. Something *was* different.

"The wind is changing," she finally announced, loud enough for several other men to hear. "Don't you see?"

At first no one could believe it, and they kept up the battle. But little by little they straightened up long enough to see that, yes, the smoke was blowing more to the side now—not straight into their faces. Any other day, it wouldn't have been enough to notice. But now everyone's noses followed the smoke like wind vanes. Patrick stood watching, his mouth hanging open. Almost as quickly as the flames had come upon them, they were beat back by the wind.

"Would you look at that!" marveled one of the men from town, leaning against his shovel. "Doesn't look like you needed our help after all."

Another man laughed out loud as they all stared at the flames that now veered east and zigzagged away from Kookaburra Station. Was it really true? Or would it shift back? Only a few minutes later, and it was obvious.

"I wouldn't have believed it if I hadn't seen it with my own eyes," exclaimed Mr. Glover, moving through the groups of men and clapping them on the shoulder.

Jefferson grinned from ear to ear, too. "Becky must've said her prayers," he said, looking at the girl. Even with all the day's heat, her cheeks blushed a darker shade of red.

Patrick knew Jefferson was only half joking. Jefferson, who never admitted to being a churchgoer.

But even if he doesn't know it, thought Patrick, *he's right*.

And it *had* seemed to Patrick as if a giant hand had, well, simply swept the flames to either side—and so suddenly. There was no other explanation. Mr. Glover stepped up to Mr. McWaid, his dirty hand outstretched.

"Well, sir, looks as if you'll have your wool after all. It's good luck for you."

"No luck." Mr. McWaid slumped a bit but smiled and shook the man's hand. "It was the Lord who spared your home for a reason."

"Perhaps."

"No doubt in my mind, sir." Mr. McWaid rubbed his eyes. "Even so, we need to go check on our paddle steamer. So we'll be on our way—"

"Before He changes His mind and blows the flames back?" Mr. Glover chuckled. "Good thinking, McWaid. But listen, you're not going to get all that wool in one wagon load, or even two."

"What are you saying?" asked Mrs. McWaid. The horses stood pawing the ground, anxious to go, while the station owner studied the wagon.

"You're piled so high there, there's no room for anything else. So why don't you and the missus go on ahead? I'll have Roger take your three and Jefferson into town right away. We'll try to get another load in, as well."

Mr. McWaid questioned Patrick and Becky with his eyebrows raised. "That all right with you?" he asked them.

Becky replied with a quick nod.

"Jeff will be with us," replied Patrick. "And Michael probably wants to say good-bye to Ibrahim."

"Ibby!" squealed Michael. "Where is he?"

No one seemed to know, but their parents waved at them as they drove an overflowing wool wagon down the station road.

"See you in a couple of hours at the wharf!" Becky promised them. "We'll be right behind you."

"See that you are!" replied their mother.

But as soon as they returned to see how the sheep were doing, they heard another commotion in the courtyard. Another visitor.

"Well, well, it seems I'm just in time!" boomed a man as he pulled into the station in a single-horse carriage. Patrick looked up to see the unmistakable stovepipe hat perched on top of J. P. Graham's little bald dome. His arm was no longer bandaged or in a sling. Patrick didn't want to groan out loud, so he smiled and turned away.

He must have passed Ma and Pa coming the other way.

"Well, there you are again, boy. I've come to see if I can be of service."

In a few minutes J. P. Graham was again the center of attention as the weary fire fighters dragged back to the station house.

"Yes, and do you know we could have avoided all this?" the balloonist boomed out to the crowd as they passed around a ladle of cool water. Many of them doused their faces with damp towels, but most turned their eyes to the master showman.

"And how is that?" wondered Mr. Glover. "It seems to me—"

"Tut-tut, my good man," interrupted J. P. Graham. "Let me just tell you the scientific value of my balloon as an observation tower."

"Tower?" asked the station owner.

"So to speak. The Americans used balloons like mine to great advantage during their civil war. Now, mine is, of course, much finer, but observers in these balloons can direct troops, just as I will be able to direct our fire fighting efforts in case the wind should change and fire should threaten your community by the river."

"Sounds reasonable to me," spoke up one of the men.

"Reasonable?" Graham strutted before his audience now from the back of his wagon. "But of *course* it's reasonable. *Completely* reasonable. *Absolutely* reasonable. And more than that, I would be happy to *donate* my services. All it takes is good looks and a little cleverness to overcome any problem, I always say. What do you say to *that*?"

Another cheer, this time even louder. It seemed the fire fighters were happy enough to cheer about anything.

"Of course," added the balloonist, "all I'll need is a little money to cover a few expenses, which I'm sure will be minimal."

Patrick didn't know why the men kept clapping, maybe because Mr. Graham at least had a plan to fight the fire that seemed to be heading in a roundabout way back toward Wentworth. Never mind that he would profit from the plan; it was still a plan—which was more than the townspeople had at the moment.

"And so we'd better hurry," he cried, firing them up even more. He checked a pocket watch. "It's now one o'clock. We'd best be on our way before the wind turns back and these flames threaten your beloved town!"

"The town?" Several of the men gasped and looked out toward the smoky countryside.

"What are we waiting for?" asked another.

"Indeed what are we waiting for?" echoed Mr. Graham as he stepped back over the seat of his wagon and turned his attention to the reins. Before he sat down, though, his eyes fixed on something behind Patrick, in the direction of the shearing barn.

"Why, that's him!" gasped Mr. Graham in the loudest of stage whispers, certainly loud enough for everyone to hear. Patrick and the others turned to see the object of Mr. Graham's pointing and gaping.

CHAPTER 16

WALL OF FLAMES

"Who?" replied one of the shearers, checking to see whom Mr. Graham was pointing at. "Oh, that's just Ibby. Maybe he was out rescuing a bird."

"No!" gasped Mr. Graham, looking very much like an actor on stage. In fact, he straightened out once more to his full height. "That's the beast who attacked me in the bush after I landed. I don't know what he's doing here, but he's the one who injured my shoulder. Nearly killed me. He belongs under lock and key!"

"No, wait," began Michael, moving to their friend's aid. "He never hurt anyone. He—"

What is Mr. Graham talking about? wondered Patrick. *I thought he was going to forget his crazy stories and not blame Ibby for crashing his silly balloon.*

It looked for all the world like an act, with J. P. Graham the showman at the center of attention. The rest of Michael's protests were drowned out by the man's shouts.

"There he is, unchained, wandering about. A menace! And just look at his ugly face. Obviously burned some time ago. I'll bet he probably even set the fire we've been battling. It's obvious, is it not?"

"No, wait!" Patrick couldn't believe what Mr. Graham was saying. Obviously neither could Ibrahim, who stood framed in the doorway of the wool shed, staring in terror at the two men who came toward him with their shovels. Mr. Graham coached them from his wagon.

"Be careful there, men. He's dangerous, I tell you. But he's not very clever."

"Now, hold up just a minute." This time Jefferson spoke up. "Perhaps there's been some misunderstanding."

"No misunderstanding," J. P. Graham insisted, his voice growing louder and louder. "This is the creature that attacked me, and we're taking him back to the law this time. Don't interfere, young man."

Ibrahim didn't wait for the two men to come to him. Like a cat he sprang through the crowd of fire fighters and away from the station house. One of them swung his shovel, missing Ibrahim but catching Roger on the back of the leg with the flat side of his tool.

"Ow!" he cried and grabbed the other man by the neck. "I'll teach you to go swinging that thing."

The fight erupted almost as fast as the wildfire had approached them, and Patrick leaped out of the way to keep from getting hit by flying fists and shovel handles. Two or three men rolled in the dirt, and the others gathered around and shouted.

"Don't let him get away!" yelled Mr. Graham in the confusion.

Patrick and Becky both sprinted around the roaring crowd to follow their friend. Michael was already up ahead, on Ibrahim's heels.

"We're right behind you!" shouted Patrick. Michael didn't turn around, just pointed at the smoke and flames in the distance. Up ahead, Ibrahim stood uncertainly at the edge of the flames, covering his face, when a horse with J. P. Graham at the reins broke away from the crowd.

"I'll drag you back myself this time," he shouted, waving a spade in the air. "J. P. Graham is running *this* show!"

Ibrahim looked back and forth from the flames to the oncoming rider. Patrick couldn't decide which was more dangerous.

"Run, Ibby!" shouted Michael, but the words fell short. Patrick ignored the burning grass and the hot spots that threatened to light his pants on fire. And he didn't know who else ran with him to the edge of the flames. But he kept his eyes on the big man, who held his face in terror before he finally leaped through a knee-high wall of flames and disappeared into the smoke. Patrick followed, vaulting over the flames. He only looked back to see J. P. Graham's horse pull up short and throw him to the ground.

"Stop!" cried the balloonist, on his knees in the dirt. He struggled to his feet, holding his injured shoulder again. "You're not going to get away, you, you . . ."

All right, Patrick asked himself, *now, what?* He could hardly see ten feet in front of his face. The smoke made him cough, and his eyes stung so badly he could barely keep them open through the tears. At least Becky was right beside him. But what about Michael?

"Michael!" he coughed. Becky held on to his right hand as they stumbled through the maze of smoke.

"Patrick," she gasped. "I didn't know it was going to be so thick."

Patrick held his free hand up to his nose and mouth, trying to breathe. He hadn't, either. But now that they were behind the wall of smoke and fire, they would have to make the best of it.

"Michael!" he cried as loudly as he could. "Ibrahim!"

The only answer was a roar of flames as the wind picked up. They couldn't tell from which direction the wind or flames came. Once again they found themselves in the middle of the firestorm. And where had Michael disappeared to?

"He was right in front of us," complained Patrick, straining to see through the thick smoke.

Soon Patrick lost track of time, just as he had lost track of direction. He thought of backtracking but couldn't tell which way was back anymore. And the flames seemed to grow hotter and hotter.

"I think we're walking straight toward the fire." Becky tried to sit down on the ground, but Patrick wouldn't let her.

"You can't rest now, Becky," he told her. "We have to keep going."

Becky nodded but said nothing. Patrick was having a hard time shouting; any deep breath he took would send him into wild fits of coughing. Still, he knew he had to keep yelling. If they couldn't see, at least they could still hear.

"Michael!" he called out. Up ahead, out of the billowing smoke, Patrick thought he saw a shape. "Do you see that?" he called out as they rushed forward. The smoke was so thick that they fell on all fours into the dry grass and dirt.

"Michael?" Patrick could barely force out the words.

A moment later they were nose-to-nose with the black-scuffed face of Ibrahim. He, too, had fallen to his knees but still gripped Michael in one thick, muscled arm. Becky gasped and ran to her brother.

"Michael, are you breathing?" She rubbed Michael's cheeks and he nodded weakly. Ibrahim didn't loosen his grip.

"We've got to get out of here," Patrick warned them of what they all knew.

"But which way is out?" Becky looked around quickly, but the smoke seemed to come at them from all directions. And the wind, which had once more sprung to life, seemed just as confused as they were. Not even the distant flames gave them any sense of direction; yellow and orange licked at them from all around, showing through the dark clouds of smoke here and there.

"This is worse than back at the house," whispered Becky, and Patrick nodded. He looked to the big man for direction, but Ibrahim's eyes were wide with fear. And since he was on his knees anyway, Patrick knew it was a good time to pray.

As they crouched there in the smoke, coughing and trying to decide which direction to turn, a dark shape came bounding out of the flames to their left. Patrick jumped, then realized it was only a young kangaroo looking for safety, just as they were.

"Wait for us!" Patrick cried, and he pulled the others with him to follow the animal. It wasn't much, but Patrick figured it was better than lying down and quitting.

At first it seemed as if the kangaroo would lead them straight into the flames, and Patrick held his breath in fear. But as the ground grew softer under his feet, Patrick understood that the kangaroo knew exactly where to go. And in the smoky maze Patrick could smell something other than smoke. He looked at Ibrahim, who wrinkled his nose.

"You smell it?" Patrick asked over the noise of the fire as they crawled after the kangaroo.

Ibrahim poked his thumb into the soft, muddy ground and sniffed. Clutching a gasping Michael tightly to his barrel chest, he tumbled forward into a clearing.

The smoke seemed lighter up ahead, and Patrick could hear the whimpering sounds of animals moving about, crouching in the hazy half darkness of the smoke.

Patrick stumbled into the mud first and whooped back at the others. "The water hole!"

The ankle-deep mud around the edge of the water hole didn't make breathing any easier, but at least it was something familiar.

I know where we are now! Patrick told himself as he sank deeper and deeper in the mud. Even Ibrahim granted them a tiny grin, and Michael jumped out of his big friend's arms to flop into the mud, too.

Becky, on the other hand, had made her own discovery—and with a shriek.

"Help!" she cried.

Patrick looked over just in time to see his sister hopping in wild circles on one foot. The other foot was strung up behind her, caught in a desperate tug-of-war with a rope.

"I'm caught in something!" she cried. "It grabbed me by the ankle!"

"Oh no—it's Michael's camel snare!" Patrick flew to his sister's side, with Ibrahim close behind. Becky grabbed Patrick's shoulders and held on, but they landed in a heap when the branch snapped.

"It wouldn't have held a camel anyway," added Michael, helping to untangle his sister's and brother's legs and arms. Ibrahim pulled out his knife from a leather sheath on the back of his belt and carefully cut Becky's leg free.

"Thank you." Becky rubbed her ankle and looked up at their big

125

friend, but he turned away and coughed as he replaced the knife in its holder.

"I think we should wait here for the fire to die down again," suggested Patrick, quickly counting the animals gathered around the water hole. Four kangaroos, a couple of koalas, and a handful of birds. Maybe more, but Patrick couldn't quite make out the other side of the water through the thick smoke.

Good thing Ma didn't let Michael bring his koala along, he thought.

Michael tossed a rock underhand to the other side, stirring up a flutter of wings, and a hot blast of air hit them from behind.

"Did you feel that?" asked Patrick, spinning around in confusion. "I don't know *where* it's coming from anymore."

Not ten feet away, smoke gave way to open flame, and Patrick felt the hair on his arm curl up in the heat. Even the kangaroos by the pond sprang back in surprise.

"The water," cried Becky, getting to her feet. The mud on her knees wouldn't matter anymore. "We'd better get in the water, or else find a way to get out of here."

Patrick looked around again, as he had a dozen times.

"We could run," he answered, "but the flames are all around us."

"Into the water, then." Becky was the first to wade into the knee-deep muddy water. Another tongue of flame licked closer—too close—and they all crouched low in the pond.

"Patrick, I'm scared." Michael held on to his hand, and Patrick squeezed it back.

"I know you are." Patrick watched the advancing flames and licked his lips. "So am I."

CHAPTER 17

UNEXPECTED FRIEND

Patrick thought it was his imagination, but he could almost feel the water heating up around them. The kangaroos shuffled nervously, almost within reach. He had never actually been that close to a kangaroo, but they all seemed to ignore the four humans huddled in the water hole.

Patrick put his arm around Becky, who gasped in short, labored puffs. He knew she felt the same parched feeling in her lungs that he did. On the other side of Becky, Ibrahim sank down into the mud on his knees. His eyes were closed and his lips moved in his own silent prayer.

"There's no air," Patrick gasped, as around them waist-high flames closed in from all directions. Even the short trees by the camel trap had turned to torches.

"I can't breathe, Patrick." Michael's tiny voice wasn't complaining, just saying what they all were experiencing.

"I know you can't," Patrick whispered back. "I can't, either."

Becky was praying, too, quietly at first, then out loud. Patrick left his arm around her and prayed along as the smoke and steam swirled around their faces.

"The birds are quiet now," gasped Michael, and Patrick knew why. He wasn't sure if the kangaroos were still with them, but the only thing left to do was duck down even lower and pull his wet shirt over his head.

"That's better," Patrick reported to the others, who had done the same thing. A moment later he heard a sound other than the roaring flames—a frightened scream he had heard somewhere before.

"That doesn't sound like a bird to me," said Becky.

"I heard it, too," Patrick replied. He unbuttoned one of his buttons and peeked out at the raging flames. Ibrahim stiffened, too, when they all heard a grunt, a wheeze that grew louder and louder in the haze. The soft ground trembled as the creature galloped closer and closer.

"It's the bunyip," cried Michael, burrowing backward into his sister's arms. "And he's going to run us over!"

"No, he's not." Patrick plucked up all his courage to stand up and take off his shirt, but he was hit full-force by the scorching heat. Even soaking wet, he felt his head to make sure his hair hadn't been singed off in the furnace blast.

"Stay down!" he ordered, just in time to see a frightened camel barreling toward them like an unruly freight train.

Michael screamed, which didn't help. In the confusion, even Ibrahim reared up in fright with an arm-waving bull roar. But the big man looked like a dwarf next to the single-humped, long-necked camel that came crashing through the flames and splashed almost into their laps. It might as well have been a dragon, for Patrick was almost certain it was breathing fire, ready to scorch them alive.

"Jump!" cried Patrick. But to where? There was enough room in the pond for all of them—but it surely looked as if sharing was the last thing on this camel's mind.

In the half second Patrick had to decide, he caught sight of something wrapped loosely around the animal's head and horse-sized snout. A leather harness, he guessed, and there was only one thing to do.

"Whoa, fella!" Patrick grasped the animal's bridle as it snorted and screamed in panic. Like an Irish cowboy, he held on, his teeth clenched tightly as they circled and splashed around the water hole.

This is a bit rougher than hanging on to a horse, he thought.

"Patrick!" cried Becky and Michael. "Let go!"

Becky dived to grab Patrick's ankles as the wild animal passed by them a second time, but she came up short and landed facedown in the water. Patrick, meanwhile, felt his fingers locked between the bridle and the bristle-furry animal. The camel's big knobby knees bumped Patrick in the back with every step, and the huge animal grunted and snorted with terror.

"You're not getting away, boy," Patrick growled through his clenched teeth, and he put all his strength to yanking the camel's head around. "Hold still!"

Almost on command, the mighty camel fell to its knees, leaving Patrick hanging backward, panting, looking for his footing in the muddy water. For just a minute the huge animal sheltered him from the flames that still pressed in all around.

Not bad, Patrick congratulated himself—until he straightened out, turned around, and looked into Ibrahim's unsmiling face. The big Afghan had also grabbed the camel by the snout and yanked him down.

"Oh." Even close up, Patrick couldn't see how the man had wrestled such a beast to its knees. But there it was, timid and quiet under the control of the mysterious Ibrahim. And now as the smoke pulled back for just a moment, Ibrahim ordered Patrick up on the monster's back with a grunt and a jerk of his chin.

"Up there?" asked Patrick, looking at the long neck and humped back of the camel. It wasn't exactly a saddle horse, after all. But there wasn't much time. With one hand Ibrahim held the camel down on its knees; with the other, he boosted Patrick up to an uncomfortable perch just behind its neck.

"Becky!" Patrick waved to his sister. Michael was helping her up out of the water, and they were both coughing. "I think Ibby wants us to ride this beast out of here."

Becky had no choice; Ibrahim hoisted her up by the arm to a

seat behind Patrick, while Michael clambered on himself. The only question was . . .

"What about *you*, Ibrahim?" asked Michael. A wicked blast of sparks from a flaming bush hit the camel just then, and the animal jerked to his feet. Ibrahim answered Michael's question with a whistle and a swat to the animal's back leg.

"Wait a minute!" protested Patrick. "What do we hang on to? And what about—"

"Whoa!" yelled Michael as they shot out of the pond, Ibrahim whistling and prodding from behind, straight into the flames. Patrick put his head down, closed his eyes, and hugged the animal's neck as tightly as he dared. Becky held on to him, and Michael—He wasn't sure how Michael was going to hang on, but there wasn't time to check.

"Ibrahim!" wailed Michael, and Patrick felt flames licking at his feet. Screaming and protesting, the beast beneath them exploded through the fire and into the thickest smoke Patrick had yet seen. He held his breath, feeling his wet clothes steaming in the blast beneath, and wondered how the poor camel would manage.

And just as suddenly as they had blasted into the inferno, they were out. Patrick opened his eyes to the late afternoon sun, and it was as if the fire had never been. The camel gasped and snorted but didn't slow down. Feeling as if he had just been shot out of a cannon, Patrick breathed clear, fresh air for the first time in what had seemed like an eternity.

"Where are we?" wondered Michael, swiveling around to see how the smoke and fire had disappeared behind them.

"Michael," cried Becky, "don't turn around. You're pulling me off."

But it was too late. Michael grabbed at his sister, who then grabbed at Patrick, who tried to hang on to the camel's long neck. But he couldn't. Again Patrick found himself hanging on to the harness for his life. Only this time the big beast wasn't dragging them through the soft mud of the water hole.

"Oh!" cried Patrick. Becky and Michael had bounced off into the dirt several strides back. "Please stop, would you?"

He had already decided that he would let go, but this time the big animal surprised him. Maybe it was the shock of the flames or the smoke. Whatever made him do it, the camel decided right there that he'd had enough. With a sigh he stopped, stared at Patrick for a long moment, and lowered himself slowly to the ground, folding first one leg, then the other, finally settling into a hollow spot between two bushes.

"Nice camel," said Michael, coming up from behind. He bent over to stroke the animal on its long neck, and the camel looked back at Michael as if he were the first friend he had seen in a long time.

"Well, I guess we don't have to worry about him running off for now," said Becky, limping up to where Patrick stood with the camel.

"But what about Ibrahim?" wondered Michael, looking back at the range fire that was burning out of control behind them. Smoke rose as high as they could see, though now they were upwind and—at least for the moment—safe.

They stood for a few minutes, watching the flames devour the brush and grass, wondering what had become of their big friend. There was no possibility of going back in, and gradually it became more and more obvious to all of them what must have happened. Patrick lowered his eyes, and tears dropped to the parched dirt at his feet.

"He saved our lives," he whispered, and the camel he now held by a short length of rope did not feel like a good trade for the life of Ibrahim. He threw down the rope, but the animal only turned his head and blinked at him with its big black eyes.

"Stupid animal." Patrick crossed his arms. "Why didn't you carry Ibrahim out, too?"

"It's not the camel's fault," Becky said, but Patrick couldn't find anyone else to blame, except perhaps J. P. Graham.

"Patrick," began Michael, "maybe he's in there. I see something." Michael inched toward the flames, and Patrick held out his hand to stop him.

"Don't go that way, Michael," he snapped. "Just stay away from the fire, would you?"

"But, Patrick—"

"I said, don't go that way!" Patrick ground his teeth and looked at his brother. "There's nothing we can do. It's too late."

Michael tried to interrupt, but Patrick would have none of it. "For goodness' sake, Michael, don't you understand? Ibrahim isn't coming out of there."

Patrick tried to hold his brother by the shoulder, but Michael only squirmed free and ran directly toward the flames.

"Michael!" he shouted. "You come back here. Have you gone soft in the head? Michael!"

CHAPTER 18

EVACUATE!

By the time Patrick caught up to Michael, they were almost to the wall of flames. Only then did Michael skid to a stop.

"Get back from there!" ordered Patrick, grabbing Michael from behind. Finally Michael obeyed as they retreated.

"I thought I saw him," cried Michael, allowing Patrick to drag him away. "I *know* I saw him!"

"We all wanted to," agreed Patrick, tears in his eyes. When they were far enough away from the flames, he let Michael cry on his shoulder.

"All right, listen to me," Patrick said as they walked back to where the camel waited for them. "We've got to go get help. Maybe Ibrahim is still in there."

I don't believe it myself, he thought. *But at least we can try*.

"Boys!" Becky didn't take her eyes off the flames. "Can you tell which way it's blowing now?"

At first Patrick didn't understand what his sister was trying to tell him. But he stopped short when he finally worked out the directions in his head.

The station is over there, he reasoned, and in his head he could imagine the sheep station, safe on the other side of the flames. To the right, he could see a gathering dark red cloud, even bigger than the flames had been. Bright, dark red—a strange storm cloud that reached miles high into the air. Even Michael stared at the cloud, for it was bigger than anything they had yet seen. But to the left, downwind, lay the river and . . .

"Oh no," he breathed, and it hit him for the first time since they had escaped the flames. "The wind is pushing this fire straight for town. Straight for the *Lady Elisabeth*!"

This time it wouldn't take long to find their way back to the river. Michael rode the camel—or tried to—while Becky pulled the animal's lead and Patrick ran alongside.

"Hurry!" he urged the camel, trying to keep from thinking horrible thoughts of burning towns and paddle steamers. Most of the buildings in town were made of wood. So was the wharf, and so was the *Lady Elisabeth*.

"See it yet?" gasped Patrick. Pain stabbed at his side from breathing so hard, but he couldn't slow down.

"Do you, Michael?" wheezed Becky.

"There," Michael finally told them. "I think so, yes. There it is. There's the town."

"So it's not. . . ?" Patrick was afraid to ask if Wentworth was in flames.

"It's not burning yet."

Thank you. Patrick sighed.

"Good," replied their sister. "It's straight for the wharf, then."

Becky dragged their little caravan directly through the streets full of panicked people, barking dogs, and galloping horses.

This is what a war must be like, imagined Patrick. He held on to Michael's ankle and let the big camel nearly drag him along. No one seemed to notice them; everyone else was too busy running and hollering to stop.

"They're all running the same direction we are." Michael noticed the obvious, but it was true. The closer they got to the water, the more people were jammed into the streets. Some were carrying trunks, others held suitcases. One woman carried a fancy white iron birdcage with a fluttering yellow canary inside, while the man next to her held high over his head a painting of an English castle. And everywhere the noise of panic filled the air, which was getting smokier by the minute.

"Out of the way!" roared the man with the painting. "The lady and I have reserved passage!"

Passage? wondered Patrick. *On which paddle steamer?*

By that time the crowd had advanced on the wharf, and people were vainly waving money at Mr. McWaid and at the captains of the other two paddle steamers. The *Lady Elisabeth*, of course, was in the middle of all the confusion, right next to a partly loaded wool barge. They could almost touch safety, but several layers of solid people blocked their way. And Patrick could only see over the tops of their heads by jumping up and down. No one seemed to care about the camel in their midst.

"Ten pounds, then," shouted a man with a fine pressed dark suit. A large woman with a flowered dress was nearly pushing him into the water from behind. "Fifteen. Twenty. Whatever you want. But we *must* have a way out of this town before the fire—"

"I'm sorry, sir," replied a man from the deck of one of the other paddle steamers. It was slightly larger than the *Lady E*, but already its decks were crammed with people and their things. "But as you can see, we're already filled to overflowing. Any more passengers, and we'll sink right here. We'll be right back."

"But you don't *understand*," argued the man, pulling out another bill from his wallet. "Our lives are at stake. How about *fifty*?"

"We'll be back." The riverman held up his hand. "We'll just take these folks to the other side and—"

"Oh, come on, man." The man at the end of the wharf raised his voice, and his face grew red. "You don't expect the river to stop that inferno, do you? We've got to get *out* of here. As far away as we possibly can."

A little man with a mule stood right in front of them.

"You can have my mule if you'll take me over first!" he shouted. The riverman only shook his head and pointed at a crewman.

"Let's go," commanded the riverman, and the paddle steamer

pulled away, which brought a wail from several people on the edge of the wharf.

"The fire's nearly caught on the edge of town now," screamed a man, running down the street behind them. "It'll be a giant torch!"

It was as if the man had yelled "Fire!" in a crowded theater. Frantic and with nowhere to go, the people packed in toward the water and the wharf even more tightly. Several women screamed, and a few men tried to push their way through from behind. Patrick felt someone topple behind him, and he fell to one knee.

"Please don't push!" Patrick called out, but no one heard.

Patrick saw the same thing happening to Becky—only she was pushed right into the mule in front of them. He watched helplessly as someone else pushed into the frightened animal from the side. The mule brayed, bucked, and kicked straight at Becky's head.

"No!" yelled Patrick above the noise of the crowd. Becky lay still and crumpled in the dust.

CHAPTER 19

PANIC AT THE WHARF

Patrick dived between the camel's legs and scrambled to his sister's side with a cry.

"Becky, are you all right?" For a moment he wasn't sure if he should roll her over and get her face out of the dust. First she was caught in the camel trap, and now this. She groaned.

"Don't move, Becky," Patrick told her. "We'll get you help."

Michael couldn't get down fast enough from his perch on the camel. Becky groaned again and rolled over to her back, clutching her eye.

"Oh dear," she whispered as she cried quietly. "I'm afraid I was a bit clumsy."

"It wasn't your fault," Patrick told her. "Here, let's get a look at that eye. Did it kick you hard?"

"I . . . I don't think so. It scared me more than anything."

But Patrick gasped when Becky removed her hand.

"We need to get you to the *Lady Elisabeth* and put something on that." Patrick checked the crowd, still pressing in on all sides. "That's going to turn black-and-blue."

"But we can't get through," worried Becky.

"Yes, we can." Michael's eyes narrowed, and he looked up at the camel. While Patrick helped Becky to her feet, Michael pushed his way around to the back of the camel and swatted its hind leg with the flat of his palm. With a lurch, the huge animal pushed forward, past the mule and through the crowd.

"What on earth. . . ?" the mule's owner turned to them with wide eyes but backed away a few steps.

"Hold on," said Patrick, pressing himself in close behind the big animal. Michael slapped the camel again.

"Say there," objected a man. "You can't do that."

"My sister's hurt." Patrick tried to explain, but he knew the best thing to do was to hold on behind the camel and keep going. As people turned around, they backed away, allowing Patrick, Becky, and Michael a clear, narrow path to the end of the wharf.

"Stand back!" yelled another man. "Let's not be pushing!"

"Watch out, fella!" Michael urged the camel forward. The big animal then snorted loudly and tossed its head about, causing the people on the wharf to panic; one poor man fell headfirst into the river.

With the first splash came screaming, then more splashes as more and more men and women were pushed off the wharf, falling like dominoes.

"Everyone, don't panic!" a man yelled.

"Oh dear," groaned Becky, but she was just as trapped as all the others. In the middle of all the screaming and confusion, their camel finally found its way to the edge of the wharf, directly in front of the *Lady Elisabeth*.

"Ma!" cried Becky, stumbling from Patrick's grasp. But even her best effort was drowned out by the screams and shouts of all the people. Patrick tried to hold the camel down—not an easy task—while Michael slipped over the side of the wharf, swung effortlessly down a mooring rope, and dropped to the deck of the paddle steamer.

Actually, he dropped nearly straight onto the heads of passengers standing shoulder to shoulder on the main deck, about six feet below. Some were leaning over the edge of the boat, trying to rescue the people who had fallen into the river. Others were simply squeezed in so tightly they couldn't move. Michael wedged his way through the people and emerged to find the ladder up to the wheel-house.

"Pa! Becky's—" shouted Michael, but a steam whistle from one of the other two paddle steamers drowned out his words. Patrick could only watch from the wharf when Mr. McWaid finally poked his head out of the wheelhouse.

"Michael!" replied Mr. McWaid, pulling the boy up the ladder and into his arms. "My boy, you had us worried! Where in the world have you *been*?"

Michael pulled free enough to point over at the wharf, where Patrick stood by the camel and the crowd. Patrick waved at his father. They were separated only by a narrow moat of water and were almost eye-to-eye. Mr. McWaid pointed directly at Patrick when he saw him, and Patrick could only stare back and shiver.

"Sarah!" yelled Mr. McWaid. He stomped on the deck to tell his wife. "The children. They're back!" He didn't need to tell her twice. The side door from the salon burst open, and Mrs. McWaid searched the crowd for her children.

"Ma!" Becky called out from the edge of the wharf, and she practically tumbled down the ladder to board the paddle steamer. Patrick followed her lead. And once they were safely on deck, their mother put her arms around her daughter and wouldn't let go.

"We feared the worst, girl," sobbed Mrs. McWaid, "when your wagon failed to show up. And by then it was impossible to go back."

"Where've you *been*?" their father called out from the wheelhouse. "I should never have agreed to let you ride in the other wagon with Roger and Jefferson."

"It's a long story." Patrick closed his eyes, afraid for a moment that his father would make him recount everything right there. "But Ibrahim—"

"Aye, I'm sure 'tis a long story." A sparkle of anger flashed in Mr. McWaid's eyes as he held Michael around the shoulders and looked down at the other two. "While I'm overjoyed you're here looking me in the face, we've got some serious discussions ahead. But, Becky, my girl, what happened to you?"

At that, Becky burst into long-overdue tears and fell again into her mother's arms. Patrick and Michael tried to explain at the same time.

"Ibrahim, he's trapped," began Patrick.

"So's everyone else, it appears," replied their father. "But what does that have to do with your sister's eye?"

"No, Pa, you don't understand." Michael started to hop up and down.

"I understand your sister's hurt." Mr. McWaid bent down to get a better look at Becky's eye. "Now, you'd better tell me exactly what happened. Right from the beginning."

Patrick sighed. "It was a mule. A mule kicked Becky and gave her a black eye. But that's not what we need to tell you."

"She could have been killed." Mrs. McWaid gave her youngest son a stern look and dabbed at Becky's eye with a handkerchief.

"So might Ibrahim," Michael yelled, "if we don't get him out of that fire!"

"Ibrahim?" Finally Mr. McWaid listened to what they were saying, and he shook his head sadly as they told their breathless story.

"I wish we could help him, boys." He waved his hands at the crowds. "Maybe afterward. But these people are in danger, too."

People were still pressing in, although most of those who had been pushed into the river had been helped out.

"Then what about the camel?" wondered Michael. "We can't just leave him there on the wharf." He slid down the ladder, slipped through the crowd, and started up the ladder to the pier.

"Let the camel go," yelled Patrick.

But Michael stubbornly shook his head and tied the animal to a post, out of the way.

"We'll come back for you," Michael told the animal as Jefferson Pitney emerged onto the wharf, puffing in exhaustion.

"Mr. McWaid!" he shouted and waved, trying to get through the crowd. He obviously hadn't seen Michael or Patrick. "Did Patrick and Becky make it? What about Michael? They . . ."

His voice trailed off when he noticed Becky standing on the deck of the *Lady E*.

"We're all here!" Michael piped up from the wharf. Jeff turned around with a confused look on his face.

"Well, I'll be—" Jefferson climbed down onto the deck and slapped Patrick on the back. "I followed y'all through the flames as far as I could, but it looks like you got here quicker'n I did. You had me worried sick."

"No time for that!" shouted Mr. McWaid from his position up in the wheelhouse. "Jefferson, you're just in time to help me with the engine. Can you do it?"

"I think so, sir." Jefferson nodded and looked around at the overloaded boat. "Looks like we're taking these people to the other side of the river?"

Patrick glanced over his shoulder at the town, hoping he wouldn't see flames yet.

"That's it," answered Patrick, "if we don't sink from the weight."

Jefferson gave Becky one last smile and a wink. "You sure you're all right, Miss Becky? That's quite a shiner you have there."

Becky put her hand to her eye and straightened her dusty skirt before climbing up to join her father in the wheelhouse.

"I'll be all right." She didn't lift her eyes.

"That's it, then," shouted Mr. McWaid. "Jeff, open the main valve. Give us some steam. Patrick, cast off the bow and the stern. We'll have to leave the wool barge there for now and hope for the best."

"Aye, aye." Patrick nodded as he once more checked the dark clouds that threatened Wentworth. He tried not to think of Ibrahim, still back in the approaching flames.

"Steam, Jeff!" Mr. McWaid cried for the third time as they made their way back and forth across the river. Each time they loaded up more and more people, while the fire on the far shore advanced closer to town.

"Yes, sir," Jefferson shouted back. Mr. McWaid leaned out over the upper railing to make sure they wouldn't crash into the other paddle steamer still loading passengers. And after Patrick jumped to untie the two big ropes holding them to the Wentworth wharf, the boat swayed and caught the river's gentle current.

That doesn't feel right, Patrick worried and held on. Their tipsy, overloaded boat took a few seconds longer than usual to straighten back up.

"Hope we're not *too* overloaded," he whispered, and an older woman looked at him with a frown.

"Overloaded, did you say, young man?"

"Oh, we'll have you to the other side in just a minute, ma'am." Patrick studied the smoke as they pulled across the river, which seemed almost narrow enough to throw a stone across.

Well, maybe not quite that narrow, thought Patrick after they had nudged into the far shore. He helped some of the older people off the bow of the boat to the safety of the riverbank.

"Watch your step," he told them, but he could hardly keep his eyes off what was happening back in Wentworth.

"Would you look at that!" Patrick pointed and the others turned.

CHAPTER 20

RIVER RESCUE

"Is he really going to launch that balloon *now*?" wondered Becky, leaning out the side window of the wheelhouse. They all stared at the big balloon rising into the air as they paddled across the river to the safety of the other side. "It's hardly the time for that."

Patrick shook his head, thinking about how the man had scared Ibrahim into the wildfire. And now this.

"The city's near to going up in flames," murmured Jefferson, "and that Graham fella's going up for a look-see."

"He said he was going to help keep track of the fire." Patrick remembered what the man had told them earlier that day at Kookaburra Station—especially the part about the city paying "a few expenses."

But there's something very odd about this, he thought.

Maybe it was because J. P. Graham worked almost alone, without the admiring crowd or many of the crew who had helped him the other day with his launch. His helpers were either escaping, like the rest of the town, or were helping to fight the fire. One thing was sure: There would be no time to spare now that it was late afternoon. Patrick could already see flames rising from a couple of small barns on the edge of the city—away in the distance beyond the downtown.

143

"There's no fighting it," whispered Becky. "Not with this hot wind. And the buildings are all set so close together."

Patrick nodded his head, and he knew his sister was right. Not even a bucket line or a fire hose was going to help save Wentworth. Only the people mattered now. And even J. P. Graham was in danger.

"Hold it down, I say!" J. P. Graham's shouts floated out over the river. "Keep that line secure. I do not want to be floating off across the countryside again." He apparently wanted to hang just above the flames to direct fire fighters. Maybe later, Patrick guessed, when the flames got a little closer, he would cut loose.

"See over there, Patrick?" Michael looked at the shore with a puzzled expression. Dozens of people still waited for a ride across.

Patrick squinted. "Looks as if the sun is setting early."

"No, not that. I thought I saw Ibrahim over there. The big, tall one."

"Michael, no." Patrick shook his head sadly. "I wish it were him, too. But he's not . . . he's not there. He couldn't be."

Night was falling, though—at least four or five hours early. An odd red dust—not smoke, exactly—was falling upon them quite suddenly, and a huge red-black cloud towered over them from the direction of the town. As if the fire weren't enough, the world seemed to be coming to a strange, dark end right above them. Patrick wanted to put his hands to his eyes and wake up from this nightmare.

"There he goes," remarked Michael, pointing to where J. P. Graham had taken off, and they watched for a few minutes as the balloonist arose into the dark sky above Wentworth. But instead of rising and holding at the top of its flying leash, as it had done many times before, the balloon suddenly lurched and twisted.

With a tremendous hiss, the side of the brightly colored fabric opened up, sending the basket, with J. P. Graham in it, spinning wildly back toward the ground.

"No, he's falling!" shrieked Patrick, running around the deck to get a better view. But of course there was nothing they could do. Patrick and the others could only stare from the safety of the paddle steamer, helpless, as the balloon basket dropped straight into the river with an almighty splash.

"Help me!" cried Mr. Graham, but his screams were muffled by the huge pancake shape of the flat balloon. In a moment the carpet of fabric had settled over everything. The basket in which Mr. Graham had ridden bobbed like a lump under the carpet for a moment, then disappeared.

"We have to help him!" screamed Becky.

"There's no one on shore to pull him in." Patrick pointed up to where the balloon had been tied. Whoever had helped J. P. Graham launch his balloon had already made his escape into the crowd, or maybe down the river. A couple of people ran to the edge of the water, but no one seemed to know what to do.

No one, that is, except a tall figure who quickly waded into the water before disappearing under the mess of the balloon.

"Ibrahim!" screamed Michael, nearly jumping off the boat.

"Michael, don't say that." Patrick had to hold his brother back from leaping into the river. "You know that Ibrahim is—"

"But it's *him*, Patrick. I know it is! You didn't see. It's him!"

"Pa." Patrick turned back to his father. "Ibrahim died back in the fire. It's not him."

"But it *is*!" Michael jerked free of his brother's hold and leaned out over the edge.

"All right." Pa pointed down at the limp balloon. "We can't move in much closer with the boat, but let's try to pull up as much of that thing as we can. Quickly, now. We don't have time for this with people still waiting at the wharf."

Michael leaned out and tried to follow the moving shape under the balloon.

"He swims like a fish," observed Mr. McWaid. "Whoever he is."

I hope he does, thought Patrick. He held his breath and prayed. Becky nudged the *Lady E* as close to the balloon as they dared.

"It's too heavy," grunted Patrick, giving the fabric a tug.

"What's going on?" Jefferson scratched his head as he stepped out into the murky half-light.

"Ibrahim's underneath the balloon," reported Michael.

Patrick pointed at the big piece of fabric, and the sky grew darker and more ominous even as they watched. Even the people on the wharf grew silent as they all watched the balloon slowly drift down the river.

"Help me pull this up, Jeff," cried Patrick.

But even with his friend's strength they couldn't pull the ruined balloon out of the river's grip. After another minute there was no sign of either man—J. P. Graham or the person who had waded in to save him. Michael and Mr. McWaid joined in to try to pull up another side of the ruined balloon, but it was hard to tell if they were helping or just tangling it up more.

Still the red dust closed in. And what of the fire licking at the edge of town and the hot wind that was chasing all its people across the river?

"It's no use," Mr. McWaid finally announced. "We've got to get back to the wharf."

"No!" protested Michael. "There he is!"

"Where?" asked Patrick. "I don't see anything."

But he heard it—a cry from the water. Suddenly the weight of the balloon nearly tugged him off his feet. A shape popped to the surface, gasped, and waved from beneath the middle of the balloon. Two shapes, and a voice that did not belong to J. P. Graham.

"Pull!" cried the voice, but it sounded breathless and far away. "Pull now!"

Michael would have jumped in just then if Patrick had not held him back. Instead, Patrick tied a corner of the wet balloon up on deck and Jefferson reversed engines. They held their breath until they finally saw two men's heads bobbing free of the waterlogged fabric.

"There he is!" shouted Michael, and they eased the *Lady Elisabeth* forward once again to come alongside the rescuer. For a moment the man in the water looked up, and there was no mistaking the face—the horrible, wonderful face—of Ibrahim.

Patrick gasped at the sight, but Michael screamed with delight.

"I knew it was you!" cried Michael, and he nearly danced a jig on the deck. "No one would believe me, but I knew!"

Together they reached way down and tugged J. P. Graham over the edge and onto the deck as if hauling in a giant, wet fish. The rescuer was next. Jefferson scurried back to bring up their steam, and Mr. McWaid spun his finger in the air—a sign for them to hurry back to the wharf.

"Let's go back for another load of people!" he shouted up at Becky, who gripped the wheel with white knuckles. "No time to spare!"

As they neared the Wentworth wharf, J. P. Graham lay on his back on the deck, gasping for breath. He looked around in confusion from person to person.

"I'm eternally grateful to whoever rescued me," he sputtered, coughing up a fountain of river water. "Reminds me of the time on the Nile River when I fished a poor, helpless Bedouin from a watery grave. He couldn't swim a lick, but there I was, and I grabbed him right by the turban. . . ."

Even when he nearly drowns, Patrick shook his head slowly, *he's still telling tall tales*.

But the story came to a quick end when J. P. Graham finally turned around and stared straight into Ibrahim's horrible mask of a face. Resting on his knees, Ibrahim was wet and breathing hard. Michael kneeled there with him.

"I *knew* you would make it," repeated Michael. "And you really *can* talk . . . can't you?"

Patrick stared at the big man, wondering if it was Ibrahim or J. P. Graham who had yelled for them to pull the rope in. No, he was almost sure of it.

Ibrahim really must talk after all.

"You?" Mr. Graham gasped, then looked around again—probably to make sure there was no mistake.

"After all you did to him," chimed in Michael. "Ibrahim saved you."

The two men stared at each other for a moment, then J. P. Graham dropped his eyes from the sight of Ibrahim's face. The big man's clothes were little more than burned rags, and his arms looked red and a little blistered.

But there was no time to explain, no time even for thank-yous. Michael disappeared into the *Lady E* to get Ibrahim a dry towel. And when the *Lady Elisabeth* bumped the Wentworth wharf, Mr. McWaid had to hurry to the edge of the boat to head off the crowd.

"One at a time, please," he shouted. "We'll get you all across the river, but if you all jump aboard, we'll surely—"

Sink. Patrick knew what his father was going to say, but it was too late to help. Like a stampede of lemmings, several dozen people jumped off the wharf and tumbled to the deck below. The boat shook and dipped under their feet, and still the people came.

"Fire's still coming," they cried.

"No!" cried Patrick, waving his hands. One of the men bowled him over, and Patrick fell backward to the deck. It was Dr. Phinneas Hume, the head-reading phrenologist who had humiliated Ibrahim on the city street only a few days before.

"Stop!" shouted Mr. McWaid. "Get back, please!"

They can't do this, thought Patrick, looking up at the people. He rolled to the side to keep from being trampled by a crowd of men who tumbled off the end of the wharf to the deck below. A couple of women on board screamed when a dark wave of ankle-deep river water surged over their feet.

"We're tipping over!" yelled Patrick.

CHAPTER 21

LADY ELISABETH, LIFEBOAT

As the *Lady Elisabeth* shuddered under the sudden weight from the panicked mob, Patrick felt himself lifted to his feet by the back of his shirt. Ibrahim held him like a puppy while the crowd ran to the high side of the boat.

"Up!" cried the big man, once more the rescuer. Fighting against the tide of people still pouring onto the boat, he lifted Patrick to the wharf above.

"But, Ibrahim—" From the safety of the wharf, Patrick looked back at the big man, who stood on the forward deck like a figurehead. The boat rocked once more, shuddered under the weight of the new passengers, then shed the river water and finally settled down. The *Lady Elisabeth* would not sink again quite so easily, the way she had several months before.

"That was close," whispered Patrick. He studied the rocking *Lady E* to make sure nothing more had happened. Ibrahim helped one of the passengers to his feet—Dr. Hume, the head reader.

"Thank—" began Dr. Hume, but he froze when he looked up to see who had helped him.

"It's the giant freak," gasped a man standing next to the doctor. "Get away from him!"

A couple of people backed away in horror, nearly falling off the deck. Ibrahim looked down as if he had been slapped in the face.

But still Patrick couldn't find the words to defend Ibrahim. Instead, he bit his lip until he could taste blood.

"Well, now," Dr. Hume finally spoke, lifting his wet shoes. "No need to panic. We're all in this together, you know."

Michael came rushing out with a towel for Ibrahim. Dr. Hume straightened his coat with a nod and a wink at Ibrahim and joined the others.

"And perhaps my reading about this fellow's criminal tendencies was . . . well, a bit premature."

"All right, now, people," interrupted Mr. McWaid as he took his position at the bottom of their ladder. "The rest of you, please come aboard more carefully."

That evening the *Lady Elisabeth* repeated her duty as a lifeboat several more times as the flames marched closer and closer, building by building. But it was hard to follow the disaster—sometimes it would roar and spread; other times it would retreat. Patrick was sure the fire had a mind of its own.

"Sorry about your balloon, Mr. Graham," Jefferson said as they stood on the rear deck. "We tried. It was just too far gone."

"That's easy for you to say." J. P. Graham kept watch over the balloon's wicker basket they had hauled up on the rear deck. It was obviously taking him a while to recover from his fright. "It's going to cost me a fortune to replace."

"Yes, sir." Jefferson nodded patiently. "But you know there was nothing we could do, sir. I *had* to cut it loose."

Patrick studied the sky as they talked. Above and behind them, he could hardly see Becky up in the wheelhouse trying to pilot them through the thick red dust back to Wentworth. Obviously a black eye wasn't going to stop her. Neither was the dust, which now covered everything—the deck, the handrails, the cabin tops. And the people!

"Oddest thing I've ever seen," Patrick remarked to no one in particular. "Dark as midnight at dinnertime."

"What *is* all this?" Michael poked his head out of the main salon and sniffled behind his handkerchief. "It hurts my eyes."

Patrick rubbed his eyes and squinted. It smelled like a desert— hot, burnt, and red.

"Biggest dust storm you'll ever see." Patrick pushed his brother gently back inside. "Now you'd better stay inside with Ibrahim and Ma, or we'll lose you out here."

This time they bumped gently into the wharf before Patrick even saw it; his sister must have guessed they were close, and Jefferson had kept their speed down to a crawl ever since the dark red cloud had dropped down on them.

"Patrick!" Mr. McWaid pointed at him. "This is the last trip we'll make. You and Ibrahim run up and see if there's anyone else who wants a ride back across. But stay close by, do you understand? Your mother will have something for us to eat, and I don't want you getting too close to the fires."

"Don't worry, Pa," Patrick called back through the once-white handkerchief he held to his mouth and nose. He followed Ibrahim back up the ladder to the wharf. "Ibrahim will take care of me."

By that time the town looked eerie and deserted, except for the patient camel that stood quietly next to a pole with his eyes closed.

Odd. Patrick struggled to breathe. *The fires seem to have slowed down.*

As they searched the smoky shadows, Patrick could barely make out the deserted stores huddled along the main street that led to the wharf. A strange orange glow, somewhere in the distance, reminded him of the danger they had helped the townspeople escape. Even the other two paddle steamers were gone, leaving their little boat idling and puffing quietly at the wharf.

"As long as I can hear the steam engines," Patrick whispered to himself, "we'll be all right."

Patrick wasn't quite so sure about the other sounds as they shuffled through the darkness down the main street of the ghost town. A cat yowled from behind a building, and a box tumbled down the street in the wind.

"Anybody here?" Patrick cleared his throat.

No one answered but the wind, and it made him shiver all the more when he could no longer hear the friendly *puff puff* of the *Lady E*'s engine.

"Hello?" Patrick tried again, just to hear the sound of his voice. At least Ibrahim kept his big hand on Patrick's shoulder. No, they would not be going far. A door slammed behind them, probably the front door of an empty store.

"What's that?" yelped Patrick, spinning around. A few men who were still fighting the fires shouted in the distance. But they were yet far off, at the edge of town.

It was nothing. Patrick quietly answered his own question. *Probably everyone in this town has crossed the river.*

Patrick took another step, stumbled, and found himself on his knees in the street. And once he started coughing, he couldn't stop.

"I . . . can't breathe. We'd better go back."

Patrick wasn't sure if Ibrahim hadn't understood him, or maybe it was just the way he was coughing. For whatever reason, Ibrahim dragged Patrick into the nearest empty store and slammed the door behind them.

"Thanks." Patrick coughed and coughed, trying to catch his breath. "I was all right. It just got pretty thick out there all of a sudden, didn't it?"

Ibrahim nodded seriously, and they both stared out the window of the shop for a few minutes. Patrick thought it felt odd, sitting there in the deserted town. And how close was the fire?

"We can't stay here." Patrick finally took a deep breath. "I'll just catch my breath and—"

Something made a scratching noise at the back door of the shop, and they both looked at each other. But by that time the wind rattled the front plate glass window so much Patrick thought it might break. Ibrahim studied the gathering dust coming in from under the door like drifting snow. Patrick was ready to return to the *Lady E* when they heard the scratching again.

"What was that?" Patrick panicked and his heartbeat raced. Ibrahim just frowned.

"Can't you say *something*?" Patrick blurted out. "Anything. Just *talk*, for goodness' sake!"

Ibrahim's horrible face knotted into a frightened knot—the same look he'd had when Dr. Hume humiliated him in front of the whole town and Patrick hadn't done anything to stop it. And when people had called Ibrahim a freak and Patrick again had said nothing.

But it wasn't my fault, Patrick started to tell himself, until he realized what he was thinking. More excuses. He kicked at the floor with the tip of his shoe, tried to calm himself down.

Yes, it was my fault. I'm just as afraid of him as the others are. Maybe even as much as J. P. Graham.

He knew it was true. He still didn't even want to look at the big man's face. But this time Patrick forced himself not to look away.

"I'm sorry, Mr. Ibrahim." It was all Patrick could think of to say at first, but then the words came tumbling out. "I mean, I'm sorry I let people make fun of you. Really I am. Michael was a lot braver than I've been. I just *let* them. I just stood back and *let* them! I thought I'd learned once not to be such a coward, but . . ."

The big man looked down at Patrick as if he understood.

"But maybe sometimes it takes more than once to learn something," Patrick continued. "Do you know what I mean?"

Ibrahim stood as still as a statue, listening, while Patrick took another deep breath to say one more thing.

"And besides that, you don't ever have to say anything, not if you don't want to. Or if you can't, that's all right. It really is."

As he kept apologizing, Patrick noticed Ibrahim's tears running down his scarred face and hitting the dust.

"Oh." Patrick stopped talking and wondered if he should say anything else. "I didn't mean to—"

Something whimpered just then from the back of the shop. They both looked.

"Did you hear that, Ibrahim?" Patrick looked around the dark store filled with material in big rolls and women's dresses. A door slammed and he jumped.

"Yeow!" Patrick turned to run, but Ibrahim held him back.

"Ibrahim!" complained Patrick. "Something's back there."

"No, look." Ibrahim's words made Patrick freeze, and his grip on Patrick's arms almost hurt.

Am I just hearing things? Patrick wondered. The window was rattling more than ever and the wind shrieked under the door, but he knew what he had just heard: a deep voice, scratchy and unsure, carrying the weight of an odd accent that Patrick couldn't place.

"Did you say something?" whispered Patrick.

"Is just a scared dog," stammered Ibrahim. A few short steps away, a small animal's quivering black nose poked out from behind a bolt of yellow cloth.

What do I say to Ibrahim now? wondered Patrick. *Do I just act as if we've always had conversations?*

"Look, see?" Ibrahim released Patrick, then crouched down and put his hand out, palm up. "He's scared."

"A dog." Patrick joined him to coax the dog out of its hiding place. Tail wagging between its legs, it finally came out to lick Patrick's hand. Its mottled brown-and-gray fur and strange eyes—one sky-blue and one brown—told Patrick that the animal was a mixed shepherd breed, only not as big as a shepherd. He had never seen such a dog before arriving in Australia.

"Likes you," Ibrahim told him.

"You really *can* speak," Patrick whispered. "But why *now*, and not before?"

"He looks hahn-gry." Ibrahim ignored the question and pointed to the animal's ribs, which showed right through his dusty fur.

"And you've understood every word we've said?" Patrick continued.

Ibrahim nodded his head and wrinkled his forehead. "He's a stray."

"What about all those times people have called you a freak or an idiot? Did you understand that, too?"

Ibrahim stiffened. "I understand everything. Is all right."

But it *wasn't* all right; Patrick was sure of that. Not after all the cruel things that had been said. Not after the way Patrick had treated Ibrahim. The dog didn't seem to care, though, and wagged his tail while he licked Patrick's cheek. Of course that sent Patrick into giggles—but only for a second—and then the plate glass windows rattled so hard, they shattered in toward them.

CHAPTER 22

LOST IN WENTWORTH

"Oh!" Patrick ducked away from the flying glass and covered the dog at the same time. Instantly the store was filled with the thick red dust and the scream of the wind. Ibrahim grabbed him up before Patrick could think what to do. The glass had just barely missed them.

"Back to boat!" ordered Ibrahim, and Patrick nodded. It felt good to hear his voice, no matter how strange it sounded. And the dog seemed perfectly happy to let Patrick hold him.

"All right, little fellow," Patrick whispered to the dog as they followed Ibrahim out into the dark street. "Let's get you out of here before your whole town burns up. Or whatever it's doing out there."

In the distance they heard the shrill toot of the *Lady Elisabeth*'s whistle over and over. Patrick and Ibrahim hadn't found anyone except the dog, but . . .

"I think that's all we can do." Patrick raised his voice over the wind. "I promised my pa we wouldn't go far from the wharf."

Ibrahim nodded, and Patrick turned to hurry back to the safety of the paddle steamer. Though it hardly seemed possible, Patrick decided it was even harder to see now than when they had last stepped off the boat. The thought crossed his mind that they might get lost only a few steps from the *Lady Elisabeth*.

No, he told himself, *this is the way*. But a shout stopped him in the middle of the dusty main street.

Actually, it was more of a cry. Ibrahim must have heard it, too, judging by the way he stopped and turned his head. They both peered back into the dust. Even the dog stopped licking Patrick's face long enough to listen.

"Hello?" Patrick shouted back into the darkness. "Anyone there?" The harsh, dusty wind seemed to snatch the words out of his mouth.

"I said, is anyone there?"

"Please, sir," someone sobbed, and a small woman tumbled out of the gloom and fell at their feet. Patrick jumped in surprise before he realized what had happened. The dog yelped, too.

"Ma'am?" Patrick knelt down with Ibrahim to help her, but she could only cough and gasp. Ashen faced and trembling, she looked a few years younger than Ma. She pointed wildly back toward the town and the flames and made a desperate sound.

"We'll get you to safety." Patrick tried to lift her to her feet. "Our paddle steamer is right over there."

But instead of going with them, the woman let out a wail and shook her head. Again she pointed back at the burning town.

"My husband," she finally gasped, fighting back the sobs. "He's hurt and needs help."

She had said enough. Behind them, Patrick's father sounded the *Lady E*'s steam whistle once more.

"Go back to the boat," Ibrahim ordered him.

"Patrick!" Mr. McWaid's deep voice sounded very far away, but at least they could hear him.

Should I go back and get Pa to help? Patrick asked himself, taking a few steps toward the wharf for a better look. *Or should I stay to help her find her husband?*

Patrick's question was answered for him; when he turned back to Ibrahim and the woman a few moments later, they were both gone.

"Ibrahim!" shouted Patrick. "Wait for me!"

His voice was swallowed up in the cloud, and he shivered at the thought that now he was all alone. The dog wiggled in his arms.

"Ibrahim!" Patrick tried one more time. He took a step first in one direction, then another. The dust was just as thick, wherever he looked. "How could you have disappeared like that? Ibrahim?"

Ibrahim didn't answer, and this time it wasn't hard to turn back toward the warm sound of his father's voice. Patrick stumbled the rest of the way back to the welcome sight of the *Lady Elisabeth*.

"There you are!" cried Mr. McWaid as soon as Patrick crawled aboard the paddle steamer and found his way to the safety of the main salon. "This dust storm came up so quickly. But where's Ibrahim?"

"He's gone." Patrick leaned against the wall and gasped for a breath of air that wasn't filled with dust or smoke. He pointed out at the darkness and explained what had happened.

"You mean he just left you?" Mrs. McWaid gasped.

Patrick shook his head. "A woman asked us to help find her husband, and he disappeared with her. I suppose he knew you didn't want me running back into town."

"You just let him go?" Michael spoke up. "I should have gone with you. I wouldn't have let him go by himself."

"It wasn't like that."

"No? Well, I wouldn't have let him go."

Patrick clenched his fist. How could he explain it? "Listen to me. He just disappeared."

"Just disappeared?"

Patrick sighed. "That's right. It wasn't my fault. He didn't ask me to come with him."

"Well, how was he supposed to ask you?"

"You don't understand, Michael. He—"

"Boys," interrupted their mother. "Arguing won't bring him back. We'll just have to wait here tonight, as long as the flames don't get too close."

"But, Ma," protested Michael. "Ibrahim—"

"I'm sure he'll be all right. But now, Patrick, where did that dog come from?"

Patrick had almost forgotten the survivor, and he set the dog down gently on the deck.

"Who's this?" asked Becky. Her right eye had turned three shades of purple.

"We found him in town," he explained, looking down at Michael. "Ibrahim said he thinks he's a stray, because he's so skinny."

"We can keep him?" For a moment Michael's face lit up at the sight of the skinny little dog, and he seemed to forget his disappointment with Patrick for losing Ibrahim in the dust storm. When he bent down to pet the dog, it planted its tongue on his cheek.

"He likes you," said Patrick, repeating the words Ibrahim had said to him in the shop.

"The poor thing looks hungry," added their mother, bending down to inspect the animal. "We should find him something to eat and—"

"Wait a minute." Suddenly Michael sat up straight. "What did you say, Patrick?"

"I said, he likes you. Actually, I think he likes everybody. He'll probably even get along with your koala. That is, if Ma and Pa will let us keep him."

Patrick glanced at his mother, who was scratching their new pet behind the ears. Convincing his parents would not be a real big problem, he thought.

"No, before that," said Michael. "What did you say about Ibrahim?"

"Umm," Patrick tried to remember. "Ibrahim said—"

"That!" Michael pointed up at his brother and jumped up and down. "How do you know what Ibrahim said?"

"Oh." Patrick wasn't ready to repeat all of their conversation in the store. At least not his apology. "He said a couple of words to me. A little hard to understand, but he can talk."

"I knew it!" exclaimed Michael.

"That's it?" Becky wanted to know. "He just started speaking to you for no reason?"

"Not quite." Patrick took a deep breath. Sooner or later, he knew he would have to explain. "I felt bad about how J. P. Graham had treated him, and—"

His mother put a finger to her lips and pointed down the hallway.

"Shh," she whispered. "Mr. Graham is sleeping in the captain's room."

Patrick nodded and quietly continued. "Well, we were in a store, and . . ."

No one slept much that night. Huddled together in the salon, they whispered and worried about what was happening out in the dark. Patrick prayed for Ibrahim and for the people of the town as he pressed his nose on a window and stared out at the dark, swirling dust. But sometime in the early morning he must have dozed off, only to wake hours later, confused.

What time is it? he asked himself, looking around the boat. He blinked his eyes and noticed what he had not expected to see for hours.

His shadow!

"Look at that!" Patrick sat up from his spot on the floor. Someone had draped a blanket over him. "The storm is past!"

"That it is, Patrick." His mother was cooking breakfast in the galley, and the air was filled with the delicious smell of frying potatoes. He followed his nose.

"Passed over some time ago," she explained as she stirred her chopped potatoes. "And before it blew away, all that horrible dust must have smothered the fire."

Patrick wanted to run outside and see what had happened, but he decided the potatoes *did* smell awfully good.

"Need any help?" he volunteered.

Ma arched her eyebrows in surprise and smiled. "Well, now, I haven't heard that from *you* in a while. Come to think of it, you *could* help with these plates. Get something in our stomachs, and we'll be able to clean up much better."

"But what about Ibrahim?" Patrick asked. He was afraid to hear the answer.

CHAPTER 23

HE MEANT IT FOR EVIL

"Ibrahim is fine." Mrs. McWaid winked at Patrick and nodded toward the wharf. "Your father's seen him."

As Patrick set the table, the boat rocked as if someone had just stepped aboard.

Good timing, thought Patrick.

"Ibrahim!" cried Michael, who had been introducing the dog to his koala in the corner of the salon. Ibrahim ducked to get through the side door. "Patrick told us what happened. We were worried."

Ibrahim nodded in thanks when Patrick brought him a bowl of water to wash in. The dust from his face and hands instantly turned the water red, and everyone in the salon stared quietly at him. Finally Patrick could stand it no longer.

"But what happened out there?" he asked. "Is the woman all right? Did you find her husband?"

Ibrahim nodded again as he dabbed his face with a towel. Patrick took that as a yes to both questions, and they watched every move Ibrahim made.

"Patrick says you can talk just as plain as we can." Michael crept up to stand in front of Ibrahim. "Is that true? Say something else. In English."

"Oh, Michael." Mrs. McWaid tried to pull back her son. "You needn't be so rude. That's Mr. Ibrahim's affair, not ours."

Ibrahim had closed his eyes, but opened them with a shake of his head.

"No," he croaked. "Is a good question."

Michael's and Becky's jaws dropped as they stared at their guest. He *did* speak!

That's when Ibrahim caught sight of the dog, and with a grin he bent down to pet the animal. "You come from the firestorm, eh, dog?" He scratched the dog's ears, and it wagged its tail. "Firestorm is a good name for you."

"Firestorm!" echoed Michael.

"Had a dog like this once," Ibrahim whispered. "When I was boy in Afghanistan." Everyone leaned closer to hear. Even Jefferson, who had stepped in from the engine room, didn't say a word.

"You don't have to explain, Mr. Ibrahim," put in Mr. McWaid. "As my wife said, you don't have to explain anything to anyone. We're just grateful to you."

Ibrahim nodded. "Is all right, I say," he assured them. The dog rolled over to his back. "I must explain."

"You're from Afghania?" whistled Michael. Ibrahim didn't correct him, but nodded and continued.

"My father, he worked with camels back home in Afghanistan, then came to this country to work sheep ranch. Saved money. Sent for me and my mother."

Though the man's English was still thick with his childhood accent, Patrick hung to every word. As a young man, explained Ibrahim, he had worked with his father in the Australian outback, shearing sheep. They had saved up their money to buy a small piece of land in Queensland and bought their own animals, as well. His father had taught him how to train everything from camels to horses.

"Was good." Ibrahim smiled sadly, recalling some long-ago memory. But that was before a fire burned their home.

"I tried to save mother, father." The good memories were gone, replaced by tears that the big man could barely choke down. He lifted his hands to his face. "This is all I get."

"I'm so sorry, Mr. Ibrahim," whispered Becky, dabbing at her eyes.

"What happened to your home?" asked Patrick. "Your sheep?"

"Gone. All gone." Ibrahim studied the deck at his feet. "Twenty years ago. Now I travel. Walkabout, the natives say. And I shear sheep."

Finally it all made sense. The man with the scarred face who hid in the barn during the fire. The wanderer who could charm a horse, a camel, or a dog. The rescuer.

"I'm sorry, Mr. Ibrahim." Patrick had to say it once more. "But what are you going to do now?"

Ibrahim shrugged and looked out the window. With the dust storm finally settling, Patrick could make out the wharf and the corner of one of the nearest buildings. Still, everything was covered by a thick layer of red dust. But as far as they could tell, most of Wentworth was still standing. Overnight, God *had* answered their prayers.

"Walkabout. Follow sheep, like always." Ibrahim nodded. "I follow the sheep."

"And the camel," added Michael. "You're going to keep the camel?"

The big man looked up at the wharf to where they had tied the camel the night before. Sure enough, the animal was still there waiting next to their wagonload of wool. Ibrahim nodded.

"Maybe so."

"But, Michael," said Patrick, "I thought *you* were going to keep it. What about your ideas?"

Michael shook his head. "He belongs to Ibrahim. But one thing, Ibrahim."

Ibrahim lifted his eyebrows.

"I still don't understand why you wouldn't talk to us at first. We understand you now fine."

Ibrahim ruffled Michael's hair. "People, they call me a freak." He pointed again at his horrible face. "Some, they laugh. If I talk, they laugh more."

Patrick understood what he was trying to say.

"You mean," asked Michael, "people like Mr. Graham?"

"Mr. Graham?" asked Mrs. McWaid.

Patrick had almost forgotten that his parents had already left Kookaburra Station before Mr. Graham arrived to accuse Ibrahim. There was no way they would have known about the latest attack on the big man or how he had been frightened into the inferno.

"You weren't there." Michael looked up with hurt in his eyes. "Mr. Graham showed up after you left, and he said so many mean things about Ibrahim—"

"No," interrupted Ibrahim. "Is enough now. Mr. Graham thought evil against me, but—"

He hesitated, as if trying to remember some long-forgotten words to a play. Something he had memorized, maybe.

"But God meant it unto good. That's all."

By that time no one could take their eyes off Ibrahim—including J. P. Graham, who had just emerged from his room, rubbing his eyes.

"You've decided to speak now?" he croaked. "And the first thing you say is that *I'm* evil?" He looked at Ibrahim as if the big man had some dreaded disease. Never mind that Ibrahim had saved him from the river or that he had carried him to safety after Mr. Graham had crashed in the bush. "That's the most preposterous thing I've ever heard."

"It *would* seem odd, indeed," agreed Mr. McWaid, "if one did not recognize the man's words."

"I don't recognize anything here," replied Mr. Graham. "This is the strangest thing I've ever seen. Why, I'm properly grateful and all for the man's help, but as I've always said . . ."

Don't say it! Patrick winced, waiting for the line about "good looks and a little cleverness." It never came.

"Surely you remember the story of Joseph," continued Mr. McWaid. "I'm sure even Michael could tell you about it."

Patrick thought quickly. There *had* been something very familiar about Ibrahim's words.

"I don't know what a Bible story would have to do with anything." J. P. Graham peered curiously out the window.

"The story of Joseph, man!" Now Patrick's father sounded like an impatient Sunday school teacher.

"He's the one whose evil brothers sold him as a slave," added Michael. "But then God took care of him, don't you remember?"

"And in the end Joseph told his brothers what Ibrahim just said." Patrick snapped his fingers, finally remembering the details and how they fit. "You meant it for evil; God meant it for good."

As they talked, Patrick glanced outside to see something familiar floating next to them in the water. Waterlogged, but familiar. He stepped out on the dusty deck, reached way down into a pile-up of sticks and branches, and fished it up with a smile.

"I remember you said you never go anywhere without your lucky hat, sir." Patrick presented the dripping black stovepipe hat back to the balloonist. "Perhaps you'd like it back?"

"Ah, my hat!" J. P. Graham stuttered and stammered as he stepped up to snatch it from Patrick's hand. "I should say."

"Maybe you need more than a lucky hat." Ibrahim crossed his arms and grinned. Michael couldn't keep from giggling as they watched J. P. Graham jam the sodden hat on his head, then storm up the ladder and away into town without a look back. He kicked up his own dust cloud as he hurried past a half dozen wagonloads of wool coming their way. The rest of their wool!

"He'll be back," said Patrick, pointing at the dust-covered balloon basket, where Firestorm the dog had found a place to explore. The dog sneezed and they all laughed.

Even Ibrahim.

THE REAL FIRESTORM

Life in the interior of Australia has always been harsh, with unpredictable and sometimes brutal weather. Floods give way to droughts, which give way to fires, which, in the continent's pioneer days, sometimes raced through communities. In fact, February 13, 1869, was declared a day of "humiliation and prayer" in the Australian state of New South Wales on account of the prolonged drought that gripped the area. People prayed desperately for rain.

The droughts were so bad that at one point a dust storm in this area extended five hundred kilometers (more than three hundred miles) from Wentworth to Melbourne, measuring up to one hundred kilometers (sixty-two miles) wide. Dust-filled winds gusted up to eighty kilometers (fifty miles) per hour, and cattle were reported invisible only five steps away. Even though a brush fire didn't actually happen in the Wentworth area in 1869, across much of Australia the real-life dust storm happened very much as it did in our story.

And the characters? Though the name *Kookaburra Station* is fictional, there really were people like the Glovers—tough folks who took on the challenge of running sheep and cattle stations across the outback of Australia. In fact, the area around Wentworth was first settled by such pioneers. They found acres and acres of flat, dry territory, covered mainly by short trees called mallee scrub.

The land was cleared, ranching caught on, and the shearers followed. Since pioneer times shearers have wandered Australia, finding work at station after station, shearing thousands upon thousands of sheep. Much of the world's wool has come from Australia. It's still an important export.

The character of J. P. Graham was also based on a real person—or a combination of people, actually, who introduced the world to the exciting new possibility of balloon travel just after the American Civil War. They were the true pioneers of aviation. And by the way, French aeronaut Professor Henri L'Estrange survived when the balloon he was piloting burst over the Melbourne Government House, disrupting a garden party. That was in 1879, just a few years after our story takes place.

One other interesting character-related note: A look back at Echuca's *Riverine Herald* newspaper from the 1860s shows this advertisement:

> *Phrenologist Hume will deliver a lecture on the practical uses of phrenology at Saint George's Hall on Monday evening.... At the conclusion, a number of gentlemen's heads will be manipulated in public, and their true characters given.... Parents can save themselves much trouble and expense in training and educating their children by having a faithful analysis of their character.*

Of course, "reading" a person's character by examining the shape of the head isn't possible. It never was. But in 1869 it seemed like a good idea to some people.

Be sure to read Book 7 in the exciting
Adventures Down Under!
Koala Beach Outbreak

A visit to the beach near the mouth of the Murray River turns dangerous when Patrick, Becky, Michael, and Jefferson encounter a wrecked ship full of Chinese immigrants. Patrick must battle the waves to save the life of a Chinese boy named Jasper. But soon it looks as if they have brought something else ashore: a deadly typhoid outbreak! Can the McWaids head off a riot before it's too late? And what is Jasper's secret?

A note from the author...

One of the best parts about writing is hearing back from readers—so please feel free to ask me a question or just let me know what you thought of the adventure. Check out some of the other books in Adventures Down Under as well as The Young Underground! You can drop me a line, care of Bethany House Publishers, 11400 Hampshire Avenue South, Minneapolis, Minnesota, 55438. I'll look forward to hearing from you!

P.S. Now you can visit me online at www.coolreading.com!

Series for Middle Graders* From BHP

ADVENTURES DOWN UNDER · by Robert Elmer
When Patrick McWaid's father is unjustly sent to Australia as a prisoner in 1867, the rest of the family follows, uncovering action-packed mystery along the way.

ADVENTURES OF THE NORTHWOODS · by Lois Walfrid Johnson
Kate O'Connell and her stepbrother Anders encounter mystery and adventure in northwest Wisconsin near the turn of the century.

AN AMERICAN ADVENTURE SERIES · by Lee Roddy
Hildy Corrigan and her family must overcome danger and hardship during the Great Depression as they search for a "forever home."

BLOODHOUNDS, INC. · by Bill Myers
Hilarious, hair-raising suspense follows brother-and-sister detectives Sean and Melissa Hunter in these madcap mysteries with a message.

GIRLS ONLY! · by Beverly Lewis
Four talented young athletes become fast friends as together they pursue their Olympic dreams.

MANDIE BOOKS · by Lois Gladys Leppard
With over five million sold, the turn-of-the-century adventures of Mandie and her many friends will keep readers eager for more.

PROMISE OF ZION · by Robert Elmer
Following WWII, thirteen-year-old Dov Zalinsky leaves for Palestine—the one place he may still find his parents—and meets the adventurous Emily Parkinson. Together they experience the dangers of life in the Holy Land.

THE RIVERBOAT ADVENTURES · by Lois Walfrid Johnson
Libby Norstad and her friend Caleb face the challenges and risks of working with the Underground Railroad during the mid–1800s.

TRAILBLAZER BOOKS · by Dave and Neta Jackson
Follow the exciting lives of real-life Christian heroes through the eyes of child characters as they share their faith with others around the world.

THE TWELVE CANDLES CLUB · by Elaine L. Schulte
When four twelve-year-old girls set up a business of odd jobs and baby-sitting, they uncover wacky adventures and hilarious surprises.

THE YOUNG UNDERGROUND · by Robert Elmer
Peter and Elise Andersen's plots to protect their friends and themselves from Nazi soldiers in World War II Denmark guarantee fast-paced action and suspenseful reads.

*(ages 8–13)